D1154013

The
League of
Grey-Eyed
Women

Other books by Julius Fast

WATCHFUL AT NIGHT

THE BRIGHT FACE OF DANGER

WALK IN SHADOW

MODEL FOR MURDER

STREET OF FEAR

BLUEPRINT FOR LIFE

WHAT YOU SHOULD KNOW ABOUT
    HUMAN SEXUAL RESPONSE

THE BEATLES

The
League of
Grey-Eyed
Women

by

JULIUS FAST

J. B. LIPPINCOTT COMPANY
Philadelphia & New York
1970

For Barbara, who is telepathic with no errant gene

The
   League of
Grey-Eyed
   Women

Chapter One

Fʀᴏᴍ ᴛʜᴇ ᴠᴇʀʏ ʙᴇɢɪɴɴɪɴɢ, in a distant corner of his mind,
Jack Freeman had known what the tests would show, but he had
pushed the knowledge aside, refusing to accept or believe it.
Now there was no alternative to belief except refuge in fantasy,
and he knew he was too strong for that.

He took a little cigar out of his inside jacket pocket and lit it,
drawing in the smoke gratefully, then staring at the match. "I'm
glad you leveled with me."

Dr. Turel spread his hands helplessly. "What choice did I
have? If you had a wife or a family, I might have asked them
first. A lot of people want the truth kept from them—a lot of

people should have the truth kept from them."

"I've spent my life avoiding the truth," he said slowly, trying to keep any bitterness out of his voice. "At my death I think I should face up to it." He hadn't stumbled over the word *death*, and he drew some small comfort out of that. His cigar had gone out and his hand shook as he lit it again. "I suppose there's no need to give up smoking now." The joke fell flat.

Had the truth really penetrated, or was this complete lack of emotion stunned shock? He had just been given his death sentence. A man should react to that, with disbelief, with terror or fear—he felt nothing.

"If I could offer you any hope," Dr. Turel went on slowly, "some change, even some farfetched possibility . . ."

"What about surgery?"

"It's too far gone for that, Jack. It's metastasized in too many areas."

"What about drugs? I keep reading about chemotherapy." Wonderingly, he asked himself how he could sit there so calmly discussing his death.

After a long silence Dr. Turel said, "There are pain-killers. After a week or two you'll start to need them. But nothing has proved effective against this type of cancer."

"What about radiation therapy?"

"We can use it palliatively. The results are sometimes worse than the cancer, and at best it's a poor stopgap. It might give you a week or two more." As the doctor talked, Jack noticed the fine sweat that covered his forehead, his constant handling of the plastic paperweight on the desk. "If I'm honest, I must be cruel. You have two months, at the outside three. Not anything that's known to medicine today can change that—or prolong it. We can help with the pain and make the end easier to bear. There are tranquilizing agents . . ."

"To make me think I don't mind dying?" Jack closed his eyes, his face suddenly drawn. "I mind it." He stubbed out the cigar

violently. "What do I do now? Try to crowd a lifetime i
months?"

"I'm sorry, Jack." The doctor leaned back, his deep
face contrasting with his thatch of white hair. "What can I say.
It's an agony for me to even tell you this. But I'm not the one
who's sentencing you. Don't make me feel that I am! What can I
tell you? Can I hold out hope that doesn't exist?"

"No." He chewed his lip, suddenly sorry for the doctor in
front of him. He could see the clenched fists, the tightness
around the mouth. A part of him wanted to help, to make
things easier for Turel, but another part reacted with anger
born of desperation. What the hell was Turel's guilt compared
to his own problem?

"Shall I try another specialist?" he persisted. "Is there any
point, any possibility that you're not up on the latest drugs?"

"I'm not wrong, Jack. I've taken enough biopsies to know
that." Suddenly he burst out, "If it were thirty years from now,
even twenty! We're on the edge of a breakthrough in cancer.
Stiener's work could be leading there, but it's too soon, too
damn soon!"

"What about Krebiozin?"

Turel wiped the sweat from his forehead. "Jack, if you must
have hope, go on hoping. I guess men must live by it, but believe me. There is nothing that can help. There's nothing medicine can do. I can't offer you even the ghost of hope. The pain
will get worse. There'll be no letup, but we can control it with
drugs. I respect you, Jack, and I've been this honest because I
feel a man has the right to face his own death. This last month
or two belongs to you, Jack. I wouldn't take it away with a lie or
a deception, and I won't with false hope."

Jack sat there in silence for a long while. Then he stood up.
"Who's Stiener?"

"A Canadian geneticist who's working with DNA. But it's
experimental work. There are others, on the verge—there isn't

time." He looked down at his hands on the desk. "My mother died of pernicious anemia six months before they discovered the factors of Castle. She'd be alive today if she had lived six months more."

Jack took his topcoat and walked to the door. "How much longer would I have to live for a cure?" The doctor didn't answer, and Jack opened the door, then turned with an effort and managed a smile.

"I'm sorry. Believe me, I know what a hell of a thing this must be for you." Dr. Turel shook his head. "See me again in three days. Make an appointment with Miss Ellis."

"Why? What will three days do?"

Jack closed the door behind him, and Maury Turel shook his head and drew in a deep breath, letting it out with a heavy sigh. He reached out and absently handled the twelve-sided plastic paperweight one of the drug companies had sent him. We all die, each one of us, sooner or later. While you could, you held off death, or you made life easier to live. If death came tomorrow or in a month, was a man any deader than if it came twenty or thirty years from now?

He ran his fingernail over the dates cut into the plastic of the paperweight, suddenly aware of what he was handling. November, December, and with some luck, January. Two months, perhaps three. He put the weight down with a grimace of distaste. It wasn't the fact of death. It was knowing when you would die. Some things must never be known. The date of a man's death was one.

He had read an article in the *New England Journal of Medicine* only two weeks ago. "What to Tell the Terminal Patient." So calm, so logical and with so much dignity. But it was all a façade, the calm and dignity of the funeral home, the scent of flowers and dark-suited men to hide the stink of death. What the hell did any of them know?

In the waiting room Jack Freeman stopped at the desk automatically. Because he had always obeyed a doctor's order, he made an appointment with the receptionist.

Outside it was a crisp, cold autumn day and he was fifteen minutes past the allotted time for lunch. He flagged a cab and settled back with a little groan. The pain in his side, the thing that had started this whole business, was still there, and he hadn't even asked the doctor for something to get rid of it.

But maybe it wasn't to be gotten rid of? Maybe that was the point—an annoying, nagging pain that would spread and grow and eventually consume his entire being. Were the months ahead going to be like that?

Two months. Two months of life. Sixty days. What did you do in sixty days? What could you begin to do?

The cab arriving at the office building cut off his train of thought, and he welcomed the interruption. He rushed into the building and just managed to catch an express to the eighteenth floor. Miss Winkler, his pretty little secretary, was fussing with the papers on his desk, and she looked up at the clock with exasperation. "You forgot about it. I knew you would. You deliberately blocked it out."

"Stop fussing and leave off the penny analysis. What did I forget?" He hung his coat on the clothestree and sat down at the desk. "What did I block out?"

"Today's meeting. The new product conference. Dr. Fleming flew in from Chicago, and Mr. Mills and the copywriters are in the conference room already."

"Oh, damn! I did block it out. Where's the agenda?"

"I've got all the papers ready and a few *embarrassing perti-nent questions* for you to ask. I've researched three of the products, and the premenstrual formulation is an old dog with an amphetamine added."

"You're an angel." He gathered the papers together and hurried out the door, Miss Winkler rushing behind him. "Now don't forget, if Mr. Mills is in one of his good moods you can

(13)

push just about anything through, but for heaven's sake, watch out for that junior copywriter, Elkins."

He walked through the corridor quickly, wincing at the pain in his side, then he paused for a moment outside the conference room. He stared at the mass of papers in his hand, then, drawing a deep breath, he pushed the door open and walked in.

The long teak table was carefully set up with pitchers and water glasses, fresh yellow pads and sharpened pencils, and a scattering of men. As he nodded greetings and sat down, he realized that they were all turned out of the same mold, all with the same dark, tight suits, the same muted ties, the same hair cuts and cautious faces—"And you," he told himself sourly, "are one of the assembly liners."

Evans Mills, white-haired and heavyset, was cut from a different pattern, but a no less conventional one. "You're late, Jack," he stated mildly, glancing up at the wall clock.

"Sorry. I wanted to check my notes on some of the product researching," he lied automatically. Then, glancing down at the questions Marion had outlined, "This premenstrual formulation, now—" He let his voice trail off as he sat down. There was a flurry of life among the copywriters as they sensed trouble in his voice.

Mills pursed his lips, reluctant to let the reprimand die. "We've got a research staff to take care of that, Jack."

"When I want an adequate job done, I do it myself," he mouthed the cliché blandly as he spread out his papers. "If the research staff had picked up the problem in the first place—"

"What problem?" Elkins, a lean, tight-faced young man with tired eyes, looked up sharply. "Just what is the problem with the premenstrual formulation?"

"That's later on the agenda," Mills interrupted. "Let's start at the beginning. Ah!" The door opened and Dr. Fleming came in, his tweed suit, curved pipe and general air of uncertainty completely out of place in the conference room.

(14)

And he, Jack decided with a sigh, is even more of a stereotype than the rest of us.

Dr. Fleming's lateness received no reprimand from Mills; his position as the agency's Medical Director put him in a different category. The meeting proceeded as usual, as a hundred other meetings were proceeding, Jack thought, in God-knows-how-many-other advertising agencies, the jockeying for position, the alignment and realignment of forces, the subtle attacks and fencing and the not-so-subtle cuts.

Mills, the grizzled bear, watched the pack fight among themselves, while Dr. Fleming (the owl?) sat wisely by and rendered judgment on each clash.

And what role did he have? Where did he belong? Surely outside the wolf pack, and yet with his nonsense about the premenstrual product he attacked first? Wasn't it always attack first— let them defend!

He remembered Dr. Maury Turel's statement. "A lot of people want the truth kept from them."

And he had answered, "I've spent my life avoiding the truth."

"And," he added grimly, "you will keep it from yourself for the rest of your life, for those brief months you have left."

He felt a sudden wave of nausea, a conviction that if he sat here for another moment, said another meaningless word, he would be violently, physically sick.

He stood up and gathered his papers together while a surprised hush fell over the conference table. He was halfway to the door before Mills rallied. "Where the hell are you going, Jack?"

He paused and looked back at them, and the antagonism and depth of feeling of a few seconds past washed out of him and he felt nothing but a confused pity for all of them. "I'm bored, Mills," he said softly, "just bored stiff with it all. I've got to get out." He looked at the papers in his hand, and then tossed them on the conference table in front of Dr. Fleming. "Here are some questions about the new products." He hesitated, wanting to

(15)

add, "Actually my secretary researched them for me." But even now he couldn't go that far. He shrugged, then turned and walked out of the room.

He felt a curious lightheadedness as he walked down the corridor to his office, but as he reached to open the door his hand shook. Miss Winkler looked up, startled. "Is it over already?"

He looked at his desk and the walls, at the David Stone Martin drawings he had framed five years ago, at the brightly colored sales chart—seven years. Seven meaningless years of boredom, frustration and—yes, whoredom! Where, by all that was holy, had it gotten him?

"I was bored, honey, and I walked out." He took down his topcoat and slipped it on, then smiled down at her. "I need some fresh air." Then, as she still didn't answer, just stared at him in bewilderment, he bent and kissed her lightly. "Take care."

He took the elevator down and walked out into the wild flurry of Lexington Avenue in the Fifties at one-fifteen. He hesitated for a moment, then cut crosstown and walked along slowly, staring at the shop windows and the hurrying crowds, till he reached Fifth Avenue, a few blocks from the park.

Passing the Plaza he hesitated, thinking of the cool of the Oak Room and the clean, dry taste of a Martini. Then he shook his head and walked on, into the park. In the space of a few feet he stepped into another world, the grassy lawns and trees with autumn foliage, the sky somehow a little bluer, the air cleaner and fresher.

He sat down on a bench and stared at the little pond with its flock of ducks. One or two months. He looked up at the trees, at the sky beyond them. Was this how he'd spend them? In self-satisfying little revolts against his job—against what else?

He thought of Anita, and as always the thought brought pain. After five years he could still feel pain when he remembered. And yet it had been his fault.

"I don't know why, Jack. It hasn't worked out—what else can I say?" She had been packing before the trip to Reno, the baby safely off at her mother's, everything arranged, neat and logical.

He had sat on the edge of the bed watching her, his eyes sick, half scared and half relieved that it was ended. "Nothing that I can say or do will change your mind?"

She straightened up. "You don't want me, Jack. You haven't ever wanted me. Why should you want to change my mind now?"

"There's the baby."

She nodded. "That was a mistake too, wasn't it? Neither of us was ready." She ran her hand through her hair and looked around the room distractedly. "Everything was wrong, from the very beginning."

He couldn't keep the hurt out of his voice. "We had some good times."

"Sure we did." She stared at him a moment, then smiled, a smile that didn't pass her lips. "You'll be a lot happier single, Jack."

He hadn't been any happier—but no less happy either. What he couldn't bear to face was that it hadn't made any difference. He had seen his little girl at first, but then, when Anita married again, he had agreed to having her second husband adopt the child, and he had stopped even those rare visits.

Five years of living alone, like water running out between his fingers, and now this. But how do you end a life, he thought brutally, that had never been lived?

He slammed his hand down against the hard boards of the bench and then cried out at the pain. He felt. Damn it, he could feel pain, he could be hurt. He had known fear and joy too— the luxury of the sun on his bare body, the comfort of bed, the

(17)

taste of good food, the agony of perfect music and the joy of women—all of it felt and absorbed, and yet none of it had mattered.

Had there ever been anything he could not do without? Anything he had ever wanted so badly that he would stop at nothing to get it? No, not really, not even as a little kid, not the toys at Christmas or birthdays—nothing that had really mattered.

He saw a little grey woman in a dirty torn coat and carpet slippers patter down to the lake's edge and feed bread crumbs to the ducks. Next to him, on a bench that caught the weak sunlight, a gaunt, drunken man slept noisily, one hand hanging down, the palm cupped on the ground.

Suddenly chill in the autumn air, he stood up and started walking through the park, heading west around the zoo and along the broad Mall. The afternoon sun cast the shadows of the statuary and trees across the path in hard black strips, black shadows and sunlight, alternating like the rungs of a ladder, till he passed the music shell and went down the flight of broad stone steps at the Bethesda Fountain through the dark of an underpass and out into the cold sunlight spilling down on the red brick plaza, a great stone fountain and an enormous green bronze angel with furled wings poised high above the fountain.

The light hurt his eyes and he narrowed them, unconsciously pressing his hand against his side to ease the pain. Where now? The plaza ended at the lake shore, two or three steps leading down and into the water. Walk down and float away, arms outstretched—how easy!

He shivered. No, not easy. The cold sunlight made death ridiculous, abstract and far off. Death was for the night, for darkness and warmth, where the shame of it would be hidden, and in the end he supposed it would come to that.

He felt a cold breathlessness touch his chest. He knew enough of terminal cancer to anticipate the pain. Would he have the guts to end it then?

(18)

Abruptly he looked at his watch. Two-thirty. But surely he had been walking for hours. What street was he at? He looked around the deserted plaza uneasily, fighting down a quick anxiety. The job, the New Products Development meeting, the hundred and one loose ends that must be tied up.

"But I won't," he said softly, the words falling into the frozen sunlight. "There are no ends worth tying up, no job that really has to be done."

He started walking again, towards the avenue. That was the hell of it, the hardest thing to bear. His life would end and no one would be the sadder, nor would it matter. A stone dropped in the water without a ripple. Anita would read about it, or Carol, his daughter, and they might talk about him for a moment—let it be without malice!

He shook his head. Oh, Christ, what a sentimental whirlpool! He grinned bitterly, suddenly remembering an evening with Clifford two weeks ago, before there had been any hint except the nagging pain. They had sat up half the night with a bottle of bourbon, stretched out in Clifford's leather chairs, smoking cigars, drinking and settling the state of the world.

They had come past nuclear testing, the Common Market, beat literature and the theatre of the absurd and he had firmly skirted around the occult, Clifford's one great passion, but had compromised for existentialism. It came back to him now how he had crumpled up the cellophane of a fresh cigar, tossed it down on the rug for Pushkin the white cat to play with and then, holding his glass up and staring at the amber liquid, had announced, "I'm not afraid of death. It's how I go that bothers me."

"You mean when you go."

"No, how. The way I act when it comes. I want to die with a gag, Cliff, go out with one big punch line. That's how I want to go."

What an affectation! He winced and shivered with the cold.

How easy to talk then, and what a lie now. It mattered. "Why didn't I tell the truth," he muttered savagely. "Why didn't I know the truth? I'll die in terror, kicking and screaming to stay —there must be a way, some way—dear God, some way. I cannot end like this. I will not!"

He came out of the park on Fifth Avenue at 72nd Street and stared around helplessly. Where now? Back to the apartment? Stop in at the office and mend his broken fences? But why? Just to have something to do for these last few months?

He shook his head. No, he was damned if he'd give up like that, go on about his business patiently waiting for the end. Why take Turel's word for it? It was all right for him to say there was no chance, shrug off Krebiozin or any new research. It wasn't Turel's life; it was his.

He looked at his watch again. The Academy of Medicine Library closed at five. He could spend a couple of hours there reading up on the literature. God knows, he had turned up leads on drugs often enough when medical directors, specialists in the field, had said there was nothing. That's what made a "creative copy chief in ethical drug advertising," at least according to Mills. Well, why take Turel's word now when his own life was at stake?

He hailed a cab, suddenly alive again with something to do, some purpose and direction. But the sudden spurt of energy, the exhilaration died away. Journal after journal repeated what Turel had said. *Final . . . no answer . . . we just don't know . . . the answer lies in a deeper understanding of the life processes . . . at the cellular level . . . genetics holds some promise for the future . . . measures that at best are only palliative . . . a genetic tendency . . . on the edge of a breakthrough . . ."*

On the edge, on the edge. Turel had said twenty years, thirty, and he had a matter of months.

He closed the past year's bound copy of the *Journal of Cellular and Comparative Physiology,* and he sat at the broad, cork-topped table. He was a fool to keep looking. Black was black, and you accepted that truth without hunting for a shred of grey.

He frowned suddenly. A shred of grey. What was the name Turel had mentioned? Stiener and his work in DNA. He pulled the bound volume back and flipped the pages. He had seen something in the May issue. Stiener, Douthright, Goldberg and Haas, "Remission of Artificially Induced Tumors in White Rats."

He read the article slowly, puzzling out the statistics and terminology. Stiener and his associates had used synthetic DNA to treat artificially induced tumors in white rats. The results were equivocal.

Equivocal could mean anything, and this was over a year ago. Had Stiener published since? He hurried over to the *Index Medicus,* pulling out the months of the year and leafing through the author index swiftly. It was almost five o'clock.

There was nothing in the beginning of the year, but in the last month an article by the same team of investigators had appeared. He copied the reference and was sorting through the current journals when the librarian, a bright-eyed, tiny woman past sixty, put her hand on his arm. "You won't have time. We're closing up now. I'm sorry."

He stared at her in a frustrated fury that left him bewildered and a little frightened. If he had spoken then, he would have screamed or wept.

"Was it very important?" she asked as he turned away.

He nodded and she tucked her pencil behind her ear. "Well, let's find the journal and maybe we have a duplicate you can borrow. Here." She took the reference from his nerveless fingers and held it out at arm's length. "August. I believe I do have one extra, or even two, here." She bustled to the back room and he followed reluctantly, looking back at the pile.

With a little triumphant smile she produced an extra copy. "There, I was sure we had one. So many people donate these current journals. No, don't bother signing for it. Just slip it in an envelope and mail it back when you're finished."

As a matter of discipline he refused to read it or even open it till he had reached his apartment and taken his jacket and tie off. Then he poured a glass of beer and sat down at the table in the alcove off the kitchenette, opening the magazine slowly.

He didn't know what he expected to find, but the article was hardly different from the earlier one. The series of rats was larger, the results "promised significant regression, but further experimentation was indicated. . . ."

He pushed the journal aside, a sour taste in his mouth, and he sat there for a long time. A handful of rats, and what connection could it possibly have?

He fell asleep after midnight, after two quarts of beer and no food, and his sleep was heavy and dreamless. Then, at three thirty by the radiant dial of the alarm he came awake, alone and terrified in the darkness.

There was some stale coffee left on the stove and he lit the burner under it and threw a blanket over his shoulders while it heated. The apartment was cold, even after he shut the two front windows; there'd be no heat for another couple of hours. He switched on a desk lamp and then, after pouring the coffee, he leaned back in the desk chair and cradled the cup in his hands as he drank, taking some of the heat in through his palms.

At least two hours till morning, till the hour he could legitimately call morning, two hours alone.

Sipping the coffee, he stared around the apartment, suddenly aware of how barren and empty it was. The lease had demanded carpeting, and he had put down a grey rug—the walls were white and bare of ornament. A three-quarter box spring doubled by day as a couch. There was a grey-painted office desk and chair and a heavy grey tweed club chair with a reading lamp behind it. An end table held the few books he was reading; he didn't collect books, feeling nothing for the empty shell once he had drained its contents.

The dining alcove, off the kitchenette wall that housed stove, sink and refrigerator, had a maple table and two chairs. The entire apartment was large, though it was only one room, and the furniture seemed unable to fill it, either in shape or color. There was a monotony of grey and white that he had never noticed before, an emptiness. Why had he never hung pictures, never bothered to get some sort of throw for the bed, pillows or any touch of color? Even the windows had only white venetian blinds controlling light and privacy.

It wasn't because of money. After Carol's adoption, Anita had refused his support checks. He had built up a sizable bank balance with no real motivation. What was there to spend it on? Travel? Possessions? They seemed meaningless. Even clothes, he had bought no more than he needed, as he needed them.

Now he could make a will, leave it to his daughter and secure her education. But there was no satisfaction in the thought. The child was a stranger.

On a sudden compulsion he picked up the phone and fumbled through the book for Anita's number. Now what was the code for Westchester? He dialed awkwardly, his heart beginning to hammer, and he listened to the ringing at the other end till a sleep-blurred man's voice answered, "Yes?" Annoyance and anxiety struggling with each other.

He wet his lips. "Is Anita there? Can I speak to her? This is Jack Freeman."

There was a long pause. "At this hour?"

"I'm sorry . . ."

(23)

"Just a minute." A hand over the mouthpiece and a muffled colloquy, then startled and breathless, Anita, and five years might never have existed.

"Jack? What's wrong? Why on earth are you calling now, at this hour?"

"I'm sorry, Anita. I . . . I wanted to talk to you."

"At four in the morning?"

"I know, only . . ."

"Is something wrong?"

"No, just . . ."

"Well, good Lord, Jack, why wake us up?" An almost visible moment of struggle and she had control. "Are you sober, Jack?"

"Yes. Yes, of course. I just wanted . . ." His voice trailed off. *I wanted to hear your voice, to hear a human talk. I am going to die, Anita, and I wanted to talk to someone I once loved.* "I'm sorry."

"You keep saying that, Jack. I think maybe you've had too much to drink." Such calm, such control. "Won't you call back in the morning." A light laugh. "The real morning. If there's any trouble . . ."

"No, no trouble."

"Then good night, Jack." And a final decisive click. Goodbye, you are out of my life. Stay out. Especially at 4 A.M. And he had never even asked about the child!

He pulled the blanket over his shoulders and bent forward, his head on his arms across the desk. If he could cry, if he could only cry!

He must have fallen asleep like that, because the sun was streaming in through the blinds when he lifted his head, but he had no memory of time passing. He showered and shaved and then picked up the medical journal again, rereading the article. Was it just his lack of familiarity with the field, or was there a general vagueness? *Results appear to indicate . . . seem to be statistically significant . . . while the data are not conclusive*

(24)

. . . perhaps . . . maybe . . . equivocal. Damn the weasel
wording of scientific writing. What had they actually found
out? How far ahead of this published paper were their real results? Or behind?

He leafed back to the beginning of the article. Stiener was the
senior investigator and the work came from McGill University
in Montreal. There was one sure way to find out. He had nothing to do today, or tomorrow or the next day. He was damned if
he would go back to the office, to that grey, blind maze, even if
there was any job left after yesterday's performance.

In spite of himself he smiled at the memory, the startled faces
around the immaculate table. No, he wasn't going back, and a
quick flight to Montreal was as easy as calling the nearest air-
line.

He put in a call to McGill University for Dr. Stiener and
after considerable routing and searching located him at the
Stanton Foundation Laboratories. The doctor's voice, distorted
by an awkward connection, crackled and sparkled, but carried
an enthusiastic friendliness.

Lying smoothly, Jack adopted a proven formula for opening
medical doors. "I'm with the Bates and Mills Agency . . .," a
truth so far. "We publish a number of medical newspapers,
publications slanted for the physician and distributed only to
physicians. I'm going to be in Montreal this afternoon, and I'd
like to speak to you about your cancer research, for a possible
cover story in our *Clinical Notes.*"

The irresistible bait of publicity was cautiously nibbled. "I'm
sure I can arrange the time." Then academic caution. "I'm flat-
tered at your interest, but I don't think I'm familiar with the
publication."

He was on firm ground there. He had helped launch *Clinical
Notes,* an eight-page feature paper subsidized by one of the big
drug houses, and he had supervised the early issues. "We're
geared to the average physician, no particular specialty. We

(25)

cover basic research on all frontiers. We like to be sure of our facts to protect us as well as the investigator. We clear all our copy with the man we write about. That means you'll see the story to approve it before we print it. I'll bring a copy of the paper along."

That apparently did it, and an appointment was set for three thirty. Jack put the phone down and stared at it for a long moment, then picked it up again and dialed Eastern Airlines. "When is your next available flight to Montreal?"

Chapter Two

F<small>ROM HIS HOTEL</small> room in Montreal it was a comfortable walk to the University. He found the dean's office at two thirty and was directed to the Stanton Foundation Laboratories. He walked there slowly, almost reluctantly now that he was so close —to what? What did he hope to gain from Stiener? Turel had said that there was nothing, no hope, and the literature had confirmed it. Stiener's work was still in the animal stage. Still experimental. How thin a straw to grasp.

A gust of wind caught a pile of leaves at the side of the walk and blew them in front of him and around him in a sudden whirlpool. The same wind sent the odor of burning leaves across the campus. He stopped, caught by the full fragrance of the odor, and stared around at the stuccoed building, tile-roofed and ungainly but made graceful by wide sweeps of lawn and tall sycamores. Below him, the hillside in terraced streets sank down to the city and the blue autumn haze in the distance. It was all so bright and clear and clean. Was it just this city or was he seeing everything with a sudden clarity? He swallowed uncomfortably and took out the scribbled directions he had gotten from the dean's office.

The Stanton Foundation Laboratory, in spite of its grand name, was located in the rear half of a basement, ill-lit and terribly overcrowded. Dr. Stiener's office was large enough for a small desk and two chairs and not much more. Stiener himself was something of a surprise. Jack didn't know what he had expected, certainly someone well up in years, perhaps the comfort of academic stuffiness. Stiener, in fact, was in his early thirties with a baby face that made him look years younger. Dress him in jeans and a sweatshirt, Jack thought wonderingly, and he'll pass for a teen-ager. And this is the man I've been counting on. He felt deflated and overwhelmingly tired.

He sat down and took out the pad and pencil he had brought along to further his story of being a medical journalist. In any case, he thought bitterly, I can always go through with it, write an actual story and peddle it to one of the magazines.

"Well?" Stiener grinned, and Jack groaned inwardly. He could pass for a teen-ager without the jeans and sweatshirt. How old was the man?

As if reading his thoughts, Stiener said, "I'm thirty-five, M.D., Ph.D., professor of virology. I graduated from Flower, took my postgraduate work at Columbia and came up here four years ago at the dean's beguiling invitation. Married, five children and devoted to skiing and horse racing. How does that do for vital statistics?"

Jack, staring at his blank pad, smiled wanly. "You're way

(28)

ahead of me. I see you've been interviewed before."

"In depth, for *Canadian M.D.* and a few papers back in the States. *Time* even sent a man up, but they never used the story. Steve didn't like him and sent him packing." He leaned back and propped one foot up on the desk edge. "Actually you picked a good time to hit us. We're really on the edge of a break-through."

Jack wet his lips. "Everyone is on the edge of a break-through." He had to fight back an unreasoning annoyance with the man.

Stiener laughed. "I'll bet, and in every field. But virology, well, maybe because it's my own baby."

Carefully Jack asked, "Virology? I thought your field was cancer research."

Stiener chuckled, "Did you hear of the white mouse whose mother didn't want him to be an astronaut?"

Staring at him, Jack shook his head. "No."

"He told her, 'Would you rather I went in for cancer re-search?' " He looked at Jack expectantly. "Well, you can't win them all. I'll tell you about the work here. I suppose you want it in a nutshell, four years of research in one sentence? No?" He swept aside Jack's bewildered protests. "All you newspaper men are the same; I suppose you must be." But there was a good-natured edge to his words.

"I'm really not a newspaper man. Our agency has done re-porting on basic science, and I've handled the stories, but I'm an advertising man underneath, a journalist only when neces-sary."

Stiener nodded. "What drug company backs your publica-tion?"

"*Clinical Notes* is our own property. We sell advertising to a number of clients. There's no one client."

"I see." He picked up a plastic pen and balanced it on the ball of his forefinger. "Well, our work has been in virology. You

(29)

know the tie-in between cancer and viruses?"

"Somewhat. They're associated with each other."

"More than that. We feel, like many others, that viral activity is responsible for cancer, not an associated organism, but directly responsible. This virus is not unique in people who have cancer. We believe that many people carry the virus, but in most of them the virus is harmless. In a few people, for reasons we've never fully understood, the viruses become killers. That's it in a nutshell, and it's not a hell of an original idea. That's why I don't see that it would make any kind of a story."

At Jack's protest, he held up his hand. "All right, wait a minute. I'll go along with it. Here, I've even got a good newspaper phrase for you. 'Hereditary Hitchhikers'—how is that for a title?"

"Maybe you should write the article?"

Stiener gave a mock shudder. "I dread writing even notes for the milkman, let alone articles. Dr. Stephanie Douthright does that. She'd rather write than research."

"What about these hitchhikers?"

"Well, where can I start? Do you know what a virus is?"

"A life form smaller than a bacterium?"

"That's well put. The bacteria have hereditary material inside them, arranged in chromosomes. All cells have this material, chromosomes. Take a chromosome out of a bacterium, or out of a cell and you have a virus—more or less. Hereditary material on the loose.

"As the simplest form of life, we could call a virus a naked gene, if you like that term—actually a strip of naked genes that produce enzymes which can destroy cellular material. They can dissolve the cell and build their own structure out of the fragments—the most basic kind of pirate maneuver.

"Viruses attack their hosts in a specific way. They enter the nucleus, the core of the cell, the hereditary material of the cell, and they disorganize it, shake it up into its basic components

(30)

and rearrange it to suit themselves. One virus enters a cell, and a hundred emerge from the empty husk. The cell is exploded, dead."

Staring at him, Jack said, "Yes. Go on."

"Well, sometimes a virus enters the cell and for some inexplicable reason, instead of destroying it at once it hooks on to the cell's hereditary material, the strip of DNA in the cell, the chromosome. When the cell reproduces, it reproduces the new altered chromosome, the chromosome with the attached virus. This new virus-chromosome can eventually fill thousands of cells, and then all of a sudden some trigger mechanism lets loose, and all the cells explode and the virus that's been hitch-hiking down the genetic road bursts out in thousands from all those cells. Do you get the picture?"

Jack nodded and Stiener grinned. "Then why don't you take notes?"

Jack looked at his empty pad. "Frankly, I am too interested. Besides I've got good recall. Anyway, you'll have some published papers for me to check with."

"A few. This stuff is pretty basic. The point is, I haven't said anything new. The virus works through the cell's DNA, because the virus is also DNA—or sometimes RNA."

"The DNA molecule is a long strip, like a ladder, made up of thousands of different combinations of four simple bases. These combinations are like a code spelling out, to the body, the way to make enzymes that can build new cells. They're a blueprint.

"When a virus hooks on to this blueprint, it shakes up the configuration, and the new cells are built improperly, the wrong enzymes may be produced, or the virus may cause the cells to multiply wildly and savagely. Then the virus produces what we call cancer. Body function is interfered with, life processes are distorted and eventually the body dies." He spread his hands with finality and Jack felt a sinking sensation in the pit of his stomach.

(31)

"And you work with rats."

"That's the work our grant supports." He nodded at the lab behind his office. "We're crowded in here, but eventually we'll pop out and they'll have to give us some room." He ran his hand through a shock of black hair. "What we've done is to synthesize a DNA which contains only one base, not a mixture of bases as nature provides, not a coded DNA such as the body uses. You could think of it as a computer tape that hasn't been punched for directions. We code this DNA with a rat's pattern. Once it's coded, we can administer it to them in massive doses. It replaces the body's virus-damaged DNA. Why it happens we don't know. Maybe it's a more labile substance, more changeable. Anyway, it causes the cancer to regress.

"That's a very simplified explanation, but I don't think you'd understand the full procedure, no insult intended. You might think of it in terms of a vaccine, but that's only a mechanical similarity."

Jack stared at him for a long moment, then asked softly, "And beyond animals?"

"You mean on a clinical level? In humans?"

"Yes."

"We've never attempted it. That's the trouble with all of you medical writers. You jump the gun. What works in animals must work in humans and ergo, a new breakthrough, only that's not the way it happens."

"You said yourself that you were on the verge of a break-through."

"We are in animals, more specifically, in rats. We've made a few tumors disappear, artificially induced tumors. You can't equate one to the other, animals to man." He shook his head. "Look at it this way. Within its limits, in the rat as we've used it, the results warrant my use of the phrase breakthrough. A very tired cliché, I realize."

"But you could apply it to man."

(32)

Stiener stood up and stretched. "This office is so tiny it makes me feel cramped. Come on, I'll show you our labs."

Jack followed him through the corridor into the three small labs behind the office. One was stocked with animal cages, and the overpowering odor of laboratory white rats pushed out at them as Stiener opened the door. In one corner, like a dark shadow, there was a group of cages with grey wild rats in them.

"We inherited those from the psychopharmacology lab," Stiener nodded. "They were using tranquilizing agents on the wild rats—collected them down at the docks." He lifted his lip in a grimace of disgust. "I can't stomach them. White rats are one thing, sweet little fellows actually. But these wild cousins— You know, as a kid in New York I used to hunt them down by the East River. We'd peg rocks at them. You'd be surprised at how many I killed. They called me Eagle-eye Stiener. Never liked them. Make my flesh crawl."

Jack looked at the tier of cages and the prowling, shadowy animals. He felt none of Stiener's repulsion, but strangely enough a queer sense of sympathy for the caged rats. "Did you ever try your DNA on one of them?"

Stiener frowned. "On one, and the damned thing disappeared."

"Disappeared?"

"Someone must have let him out of the cage. Steve said he became a snake and wriggled out. I wonder what the psych boys would say about that? This is our radiation lab."

He opened the central door and pointed out, with justifiable pride, the massive electronic equipment that lined the walls. "We may look pretty shabby on the outside, but there's fifty thousand bucks' worth of grant money stacked up in this room alone."

The third room was set up as a biochemistry laboratory with two lead-topped tables under shelves of glassware and reagent bottles. The tables were covered with a bewildering array of equipment. A handsome, grey-eyed woman in her late thirties was working at the table. She had close-cropped, sandy hair and a glowing complexion that scorned cosmetics. When Jack came in she was titrating a colorless liquid into a glass dish filled with reagent, and as she reached the end point, the solution slowly turned pink. Shutting off the valve, she reached for a pack of cigarettes and grinned at them.

"Steve, this is Mr. Freeman, a medical writer from New York. This is my associate, Dr. Stephanie Douthright, a biochemist, and a good one too."

"The best in the business." She lit a cigarette and inhaled gratefully, then let the smoke trickle out. "That's better." She squinted at the titration apparatus and jotted down the fluid level, then turned to the men. "My first cigarette for the day."

"But not your last," Stiener frowned. "I thought the doctor told you to lay off."

"What the hell does he know? All right, relax. So I get me a cancer. You can shoot me full of DNA and I'll be as good as new. You said you needed a human volunteer." She boosted herself up on the table edge. "What kind of a story is he doing? Boy scientist cracks the genetic barrier or hereditary hitchhiker?"

She broke into laughter at Jack's startled look. "So he fed you that old one? I'm ashamed of you. He's been trying to palm off that title on every science writer who's ever been up here."

Embarrassed, Stiener said, "If you weren't so damned good, I'd bounce you on your butt."

She laughed again, a hearty guffaw, and reached out to rumple Stiener's hair as he ducked out of reach. "He just talks like that because he means it. Have you got your story?"

"Some of it. We were talking about using the method in humans."

Steve looked at Stiener sharply. "What did you tell him about that?"

Stiener's face was troubled. "I told him that what works in

animals doesn't necessarily work in humans. You can't equate one to the other."

"The hell you can't." Steve ground out her half-smoked cigarette. "I've told you a dozen times that we're sitting on a powder keg. All we need is some experimental work in humans."

"Steve!" Stiener's voice was suddenly hard. "Mr. Freeman is a journalist. What is released for publication in this lab will be released by me."

She stared at him challengingly for a moment, then looked away and reached for the pack of cigarettes again. Her fingers were steady as she took one out, but her lips were tight.

Jack had been following the exchange eagerly. There was something here that built up his hopes. Stiener was cautious, correctly so. But had they tried it yet? Were they telling him the whole story?

"But you are set up for human experimentation?" he asked carefully.

"Set up? We have the DNA. We've even coded batches for humans. We know how to inject it—what other setup is necessary? That's not what holds me back," Stiener said with a frown. "Do you know what happened in the States when they started testing Krebiozin?"

Steve snorted. "You're not comparing this to Krebiozin?"

"Of course not. This has no relationship to Krebiozin and we know it. It's the manner of testing. I'm not eager to be branded a charlatan."

"But if you had a terminal cancer case," Jack interrupted, "someone who was going to die in a few months . . . wouldn't you try it then?"

"We haven't enough for a controlled study. One man—that would prove nothing."

"Except to the man," Steve murmured. Jack turned to her, and then back to Stiener.

"I am a writer," he said slowly, his heart beginning to race..

This was the gamble. "I work for the agency that puts out *Clinical Notes,* but I didn't come up here to do a story. Not for *Cinical Notes* or any other publication."

Stiener stared at him, scowling, as he went on slowly. "I—I want to tell you the truth." He looked around for a chair and pulled out a bench stool, almost collapsing on it. "I came up here because I saw your name on an article in a medical journal."

"The story . . ."

"The story was a hoax, to get me in here."

"An expensive hoax."

"I've thirty thousand dollars and no wife or children. Plane flight up here isn't so much, especially to a man with two months to live."

It was a bombshell, and he knew it. Stiener's head came up as his eyes widened. Steve slid off the bench to her feet. "Two months?" Stiener asked. "What do you mean?"

Jack took out a little cigar and unwrapped it. He cupped a match and bent to its flame, then straightened up. "I'm a terminal cancer case with two months to live. Gastric cancer, and it's inoperable, I've been told. It's metastasized throughout my body." The words, so calm and devoid of emotion were like coals in his mouth. "I have no family, no attachments and I'm afraid to die."

"We all die," Stiener said softly.

"In twenty years, ten years, a year, but none of us knows when. That doesn't matter. What matters is that there's no earthly reason why I shouldn't be your first case. What do you say to that?"

There was a long silence. The cold sunlight of the late afternoon lanced into the laboratory and shattered into color as it touched the glassware. Very quietly Stiener said, "I'd say we should have a drink, a long, serious drink."

(36)

Chapter Three

THE BAR OF THE ROYAL EDWARD was dark with atmosphere, from the burnished wooden beams to the heavy stained-oak benches and booths. A few dim, amber highlights gleamed off the polished brass mugs on the wall, but failed to do more than accent the darkness.

Jack, at one of the booths, turned his glass of Canadian whiskey absently, staring across the table at Stiener and Steve. Stiener, his voice heavy, was repeating what he had already told Jack a dozen times. "I cannot jump to human experiments. I haven't even established an LD_{50} in mice. How can I extrapolate dosage?"

"Your lethal dose doesn't matter. Don't you understand that nothing matters? I'm a dead man. There's nothing to lose."

"There are laws about human trials of drugs, new drugs."

"Item one," Steve said, stirring her drink with her finger. "DNA isn't a new drug. Item two: This is Canada, not the States. Item three: Who's to know?"

Stiener tossed a swizzle stick across the table. "Use this. That's a disgusting habit."

She grinned at him, lifting on eyebrow. "You're hostile."

"You're drunk." Stiener chewed his lip. "How do I know it will be specific for gastric cancer? Or even touch it? We've only tried it in artificial tumors in mice, a tumor that has not metastasized."

Jack sighed. They had been over this along with every possible objection that Stiener could raise, and as each was answered he went to another. They had been sitting here drinking for hours, arguing in a circle around what to him was a simple, basic point. He was sick. The drug spelled a chance of help. There was nothing to lose. Why not use it?

He felt an overwhelming wave of tiredness, and deep in his gut the nagging ever-present pain. Why fight? What did it matter? What was he chasing? Why?

Stiener was afraid with a fear born out of years of training. The drug showed promise in animals. He couldn't predict its action in humans. He was a researcher, not a clinician. It must be worked up gradually, cautiously, in an orthodox way, in a controlled way.

Looking at his watch, he stood up suddenly. "I'm an hour late. Martha will start worrying." He looked down at Jack indecisively, searching for words that didn't exist. "I'm sorry." Then abruptly he turned and hurried out of the bar. Steve looked after him cynically. "Now do you think that was just a way to beat the check?"

(38)

Jack sighed. "I don't know, but I think I'd like another drink."

Steve signalled the waiter. "Make it four, two gins and bitters and two of those lousy Canadian boozes for him." She stared across the table at Jack, her sandy, short-cropped hair and square face suddenly softened by the dim light. "We can at least get drunk."

"There's a world of philosophy in you, Steve." He finished the glass of whiskey quickly and sighed. "Tell me, how did a nice kid like you get into a racket like this?"

Steve let out a bellow of laughter. "I like you. Finish up and I'll show you my garden."

"That's a new one. It used to be etchings when I was young—when we were both young—that must have been a million years ago."

"Speak for yourself, sonny."

They had another round and then, warm and high, they left the bar. Outside the sun was low above the city and the air had turned cold. Jack could feel the liquor spread through him. On an empty stomach he'd really feel this!

As if reading his thoughts, Steve said, "Let's get some food into us. Come on over to my place. It's only a few minutes away. I'll scramble some eggs."

Jack nodded and Steve took his arm as they walked. "I've got some feminine vestiges yet."

He started to protest and then shook his head. "I don't know. I'm too high to tell." The drinks were like a barrier between himself and the world. He had come here on a last, slim hope. Now it was gone. So what? Find another "cure for cancer"? Search for a quack? Or maybe, he thought bitterly, just stay drunk. At least it made thinking harder and he didn't have to worry about becoming an alcoholic.

Steve's home was a small, two-storied house, squeezed in between an apartment building on one side and a store on the other. "I rent the whole thing," she told him, opening the door and switching on the light. "The whole damn house is only twelve feet wide. I've got a living room and kitchen downstairs and a bedroom upstairs—and my garden."

The living room was a surprise, a completely feminine room with organdy curtains, frilly lampshades and flowered wall paper. Steve grinned at his expression. "That's Rhoda's doing."

"Rhoda?"

"My . . ." Steve hesitated. "My roommate. You'll meet her later. Make yourself to home and I'll rassle up some grub." She threw off her jacket and went through to the kitchen where a clatter of pots and pans announced her progress. Jack touched the couch and then pushed the organdy curtains aside and peered out. There was an alley alongside the house, and beyond it the vague shadows of a garden.

"Help yourself to some booze," Steve shouted. "There's a bottle and glasses on the sideboard."

He mixed a stiff drink and then wandered into the kitchen, searching for ice. She had set two places at the small table and was taking the eggs off the stove. "Sit down. You're just in time."

The eggs were good and the coffee was perfect. Filled, he sat back and lit one of his cigars. "Well, where do I go from here?"

Steve stared at him speculatively. "You let Stiener off the hook. He was defensive, and maybe if you had pushed real hard —I don't know."

"Will he change his mind?"

"No. He'll have time to come up with a dozen other reasons to justify himself. A nice guy. Sweet, but scared as hell of the label quack." She lit a cigarette and inhaled deeply. "It's the nature of the beast, of this kind of research. You get burned pretty often with the wrong kind of publicity and every doctor is ready to jump on you."

"Steve, tell me on the level, is there a chance that his DNA could help in my kind of cancer?"

She chewed her lower lip. "I don't know. Maybe there's a chance; maybe not. If the cancer is viral as he's convinced all cancer is—I'm not so sure, if the artificial DNA replaces it, if your own body cells aren't harmed by the DNA, if—so damn many ifs. How can anyone say? We're truly groping in the dark."

He sat there, looking down at his plate for a long time. Then suddenly Steve stood up. "Come on, let's look at my garden."

She led him through the kitchen door and down the narrow alley to the rear of the house. The garden was a twelve-foot square, a typical city house backyard surrounded by a tall wooden fence. It was dark, but there was almost a full moon and with that, plus the light that spilled out of the kitchen window, Jack could see the garden, not clearly, but with enough detail to make him gasp.

There were a half dozen trees and twice that many shrubs, all overgrown and distorted into wild, nightmarelike caricatures. Every branch and trunk had misshapen galls and protuberances, wild excrescences bulging out of the bark, and from these startling growths shot up and down and out.

Blossoms grew where they had no reason to, and roots, trunks and leaves seemed confused and disorganized. It was a garden of insanity, of wild, unrestrained growth without rhyme or reason, and it made Jack wince and unconsciously draw back.

"Like 'em?"

"What the hell are they?"

"Take a look. They won't bite."

He walked forward and examined what looked like the misshapen figure of a maple tree. Only a handful of leaves were five-pointed; most were long and tapering, some like ferns. For every stiff branch there was one that drooped and swayed in the breeze, almost with a motion of its own. Here and there along the stems, flowers bloomed, no two alike.

He shook his head, and wandered to another bush, again a travesty of nature or a miracle of grafting. Different flowers ranging through every color of the floral spectrum bloomed along the stems. Farther along, a tall, slim birch sported a mosaic of varicolored bark, and at the far end of the garden a weeping willow drooped with deep, unmistakably blue leaves.

He shook his head, turning back to Steve in amazement. "It looks as if you managed to graft stuff no one else ever has, unless they're artificial. They look like those crazy plastic flowers."

Steve snorted. "Go ahead, pick one."

He picked a roselike blossom of pale lavender, as large across as his hand. It was real and its fragrance was disturbingly familiar. "Milkweed, but it doesn't look like milkweed, and there's no sap."

"It isn't milkweed, or some of it isn't. That's interesting. I never thought of milkweed. I'll have to take another look at its chromosomes."

"What did you graft it from?"

"Graft, hell. I grew them all." She gestured at the entire garden. "Every damned one grew, and they were all normal to begin with."

"How did you do it?"

"Plant DNA." She grinned crookedly. "It looks mysterious, but it's all very simple. What determines what a seed will grow into? What keeps a tree a tree? Or better still, a birch tree a birch tree?"

Jack inhaled the cloying odor of the blossom. "Chromosomes, I guess."

"You guess right," she said mockingly. "Its chromosomes, or since chromosomes are only long threads of DNA molecules, its DNA, its own particular kind of DNA or RNA, whichever molecule its chromosomes are made of."

(42)

"And you can control the DNA of the tree?"

"Control?" She considered that a moment. "Let's say I can shake it up, bewilder it. In effect I can feed milkweed chromosomes to a birch tree and confuse it, make it grow milkweed blossoms whether it wants to or not."

"I don't understand that."

"Why should you understand it? It's never been done before. If I fed the DNA to a rose bush, I could change it into a cabbage plant."

"You've only tried it with plants?"

She took the blossom from him and started tearing off the petals. "He changes. He changes not. He changes— No, I tried it on one of Stiener's rats, his wild rats. The damned thing changed into a snake when I tried to take it out of the cage. I'm still pretty much of a woman, I guess. I screamed and dropped it and it wriggled away."

"It really changed into a snake?" He tried to see her eyes, to tell if she was teasing him.

"Yes, a snake!" She shrugged and threw away the plucked flower head. "We are what we are only because every one of our cells carries the pattern of our body, carries it in its DNA. Change the DNA, change the pattern, inject new DNA, and our body has the potential to change. Lycanthropy. Man into wolf. Maybe they knew about DNA in the old days and called it a magical potion. Feed a man the right potion and he can change into a wolf."

"You don't believe that?"

She looked up at him, her eyes expressionless, her face tight for a long moment. "I believe in what I do," she said finally. "I believe I've changed these flowers. I believe that rat became a snake. I believe I'm thirsty as hell. Come on back in. I'm cold."

Inside the room she poured two more drinks and slumped down in a chair, her feet up on a table. Jack sat across from her. "I grew them all," she said slowly, "and they change from day to

(43)

day. Rhoda calls it my Martian garden. It's lousy with plant viruses, with every kind of DNA and RNA I've been able to synthesize."

"What are you trying to do?"

She shrugged. "I don't know. I've achieved plasticity, but I have no control. Maybe I'm trying for the flower of the future, controlled evolution through nucleic acids—maybe I'm just trying to get in with the faculty wives' local garden club. I exhibited one of my plants once and was treated very coldly."

"You at a garden club? It doesn't seem right."

"I have a lot of surprising qualities. I have mental abilities you couldn't even guess at." She looked at her drink moodily. "Maybe I'm just trying to duplicate the apple Eve picked. You think that was just a plain apple, Jack . . . Hey, that's good! Applejack."

"Steve." He leaned forward. "What can I do about Stiener?"

"Not a cotton-pickin' thing. You're in a quandary, friend." She sipped her drink slowly. "Stiener won't budge—and you don't want to die."

"Who does?" The liquor was easing some of the tension out of him. "Not just yet. Steve, I don't think I ever lived, and all of a sudden it's come home to me." He swirled the liquor in the glass. "I think this is the answer. Maybe I should just stay drunk."

"Maybe, or maybe you should butter me up a bit. I have access to all of Stiener's files and material."

He looked at her slowly, appraisingly, for a long time, and she stared back, her grey eyes half-closed, the irises almost continuous with the pupil, a strange luminous grey. Her face was immobile.

"What do you want, Steve? If it's money—"

Her mouth twisted with quick scorn. "Just like a man. Money!"

"I'm sorry. You said—"

"I said, 'Butter me up.' Don't insult me." She finished her drink and reached for the bottle. "One more. Maybe I want you, Jack."

He tried to laugh. "It's a hell of a deal if you do."

All at once she grinned. "But it's a deal, okay? And I collect when I want to. If you're around to collect."

"You're kidding."

"I'm serious. Is it a deal?"

He wet his lips and nodded. "It's a deal."

"You'd sell your soul for that life, wouldn't you?"

Goaded, he said, "Wait till your turn comes."

She winced. "I deserved that." There was the ring of the doorbell, and she jumped up. "That's Rhoda. We can go now. I was waiting for her to get home."

She hurried into the hall and Jack heard whispered voices, low at first and then rising slowly, and finally Steve's, suddenly audible. "I said yes, that's all." There was a pause, then Steve came into the room and behind her, Rhoda.

Jack stood up and caught his breath. He wasn't sure of what he had been expecting, but certainly not this. The girl behind Steve was tall, almost his own height, slim and yet rounded. Her dark blond hair was parted in the middle and held back carelessly with a silver clasp, but the very carelessness, almost too casual not be affected, lent a classic simplicity to her face. Her features too were classic, her cheekbones high, her chin squared and her nose narrow and straight with no indentation at the brow.

But it was her eyes that caught Jack and held him. They were wide, so wide that even the dark, heavy lashes failed to narrow them. They were grey, like Steve's, yet paler than any eyes he had ever seen.

He stood like that, staring almost rudely, until Steve laughed and put an arm around Rhoda. "I want you to meet Jack whose days are numbered."

(45)

Rhoda frowned. "You have one hell of a sense of humor, black humor." Her voice was low and rich. "I'm Rhoda Watson." She held her hand out with a disarming directness. Her fingers were cool and firm in his grasp.

"I'm Jack Freeman."

"I know." She smiled, her face quickly alive and eager. Turning to Steve, she said, "Go ahead. I'll keep the home fires burning."

Jack followed Steve from the house. "I don't understand. Where are we going?"

"To the lab." Steve's stride was free and quick. "I'm going to shoot you full of DNA plus and see if that quack, Steiner, has a real cure for cancer."

"Then you're going to do it? You'll give me the treatment?"

"Was there ever any doubt?"

"But why, Steve?"

She stopped abruptly. "We made a deal. Let that be reason enough, or say that when a man is in need of treatment, a scientist who can offer it shouldn't refuse . . . or just say I have my own dark reasons." She started to walk again. "I may not be as generous as I seem. Let me tell you this, and then forget it. You don't know quite what you are or what I want to make you."

"I don't understand."

"Of course you don't." At the lab she used a passkey. Stopping at Stiener's desk, she nodded to the back lab. "You go in there and take your jacket and shirt off. I'll be right along. I have some—paper work to do."

He had stripped down to his pants when she came back. Quickly and efficiently she took a beaker out of the refrigerator and set it over a Bunsen flame. Unwrapping a sterile thermometer, she placed it in the beaker and then took a packaged syringe and needle out. "You're lucky we have one this size. We were doing blood cultures last week."

(46)

She checked the thermometer, turned the flame off and carefully filled the syringe. Holding it to the light, she worked the plunger up till the air was exhausted and a drop of fluid ran down the needle.

She balanced the syringe on the beaker and soaked a wad of cotton in alcohol. "Hold out your arm."

With a forced smile he said, "Practicing medicine without a license?"

"I started as a registered nurse." She slipped a length of tubing around his upper arm, then looked at him speculatively. "You're nicely preserved for your age. Single?"

"Divorced."

She grinned wolfishly. "Same thing." She patted his chest with a proprietary air.

"For Christ's sake, get on with it!"

"Temper." Still smiling, she lifted the syringe and with a quick, deft movement slipped the needle into his vein. As a feather of blood backed into the liquid in the syringe, she pulled the tourniquet off. "All right. Now we let it in slowly. It should take a couple of minutes." She looked up at him. "You're sweating."

"Wouldn't you be?"

"I guess I would. You know what this is supposed to do?"

"Vaguely. What I hope it will do is give me a chance to live."

"Maybe. According to Stiener's theory it should replace your own DNA in susceptible cells. It should replace the virus and the DNA, shake up the cells and then let your own body take over."

"Susceptible cells?"

"Carcinogenic cells, tumor cells, cancer cells. Of course, in our rats we created the cancers and maybe those tumors were more susceptible. But there's still a good chance. The blood should carry this to every cell in your body, normal or malignant. If I

(47)

didn't think there was a chance, Jack, I'd never have taken the risk of doing this. More than just a chance as far as I'm concerned."

With maddening slowness the syringe emptied, and finally the plunger reached the end of the barrel. Steve put a pledget of cotton over the needle and pulled it out. "There. How did that feel?"

He flexed the arm, holding the pledget. "It hurts like hell all through the arm."

"It will hurt more in a few hours," she said softly. "I never told you what the rats go through. It may hurt more than the cancer ever would."

"I can take it."

"Tough boy! Put your shirt on."

He was starting to button it up when he heard the front door slam, and then Stiener's sharp voice called out, "Who's there?"

"Oh, Christ!" Steve began to gather up the syringe and beaker, but then with a shrug let them lie and turned to the door as Stiener came into the lab.

Chapter Four

W‍HAT'S GOING ON HERE, Steve?" Stiener asked, looking around the room.

"If you say, 'What's the meaning of this?' I'll scream." She fumbled for a cigarette and a match. "I just gave Freeman a massive dose of our special DNA." She was trying to keep her voice level, but there was a hard edge to it.

"You just what?" Stiener's eyes went from the needle and the beaker to Jack's arm and unbuttoned shirt. "What the hell do you mean, you gave him a dose of DNA?"

Steve wet her lip. "It's as simple as ABC. A man has cancer. We have a possible cure. I gave it to him."

"You did? Since when are you running this lab?"

"I'm sorry, I guess. But since you wouldn't do it."

"Where in hell do you come off . . ."

"All right!"

"Taking this into your own hands? Did you have any records on him, any biopsy? Has he really got cancer? What do you know about him? Have you seen his medical report?"

Steve's air of assurance crumbled before his onslaught. "All right. I let the clinical elements go. I was only concerned with the human. Goddam it, the man is dying."

"Sure, and what if you've caused his death two months sooner with a miscalculated dose? What do you tell the police?"

"My death is a fact," Jack put in. "I had no chance of living."

Stiener brushed the protest aside, his voice savage. "I don't know that. Steve doesn't know that. We've seen no medical reports, done no examination. How do we know you're not some crackpot? What do we know about you except that you lied to get in here? That's a hell of an introduction!"

Desperately Jack said, "You're making a big thing out of this. Steve took no chance, except a chance to help me. Sure I lied to get in, but if I hadn't, how far would I have gotten? You've only got to pick up that phone and call New York, speak to my doctor to confirm the truth. The fact of my cancer is a truth."

"You're drunk," Stiener said coldly, "and you are too, Steve, but you've gone too damned far this time." His voice rose and his face grew white, then flushed. "By what right dared you do anything like that, drunk or sober? Of all the stupid and unethical . . . What are you trying to do, crucify me? If you think for one minute I'm going to allow this . . ."

"Stop, please." She drew in a deep breath of smoke and let it out slowly. "You've made your point."

"Not by a long shot I haven't. You're through here, Steve."

"I was through even if you didn't catch me," she said levelly.

"I've got some sense of ethics left. I know just what I did and all the implications of it. I left a predated note of resignation on your desk, also another note that absolves you from any blame in case—Jack dies. I made it clear that I did this underhanded, illegally and without your knowledge. There'll be no trouble for you no matter what happens. Only—" She caught her lip. "I'm sorry. Christ, I'm sorry it had to be this way."

Some of the tightness left Stiener, and his voice took on a querulous note. "Why, Steve? Why? That's what I can't understand. Why would you do anything like this? You're too careful, too much of a scientist. I don't understand."

"Why?" She looked at Jack and then at Stiener and suddenly, irrelevantly, Jack noticed how wide her eyes were, how wide and colorless. "Because of reasons beyond either of you. What do you know about loneliness, of year after year without an answer, knowing there can't be an answer—"

"You're not making sense," Stiener said impatiently. "You're drunk."

"No, I'm not. You asked why." She shook her head. "Because I will not stand by and see a man die. Is that reason enough, sober reason? Because I'm sick to death of being alone, but you won't understand that, and I can't begin to explain. I did something you feel I shouldn't have done. Let's leave it at that. If you want to prosecute me, you know where to find me." She turned to Jack. "Button your shirt," she snapped, "and stop standing there like an idiot." She grabbed her cigarettes and brushed past the two men, out of the lab.

Jack watched her go in bewilderment, then turned to Stiener, but neither of them said anything. The pain had spread from his arm to his shoulder, a dull, burning pain. He buttoned his shirt and took his jacket.

"Where are you going?" Stiener said suddenly, mildly.

"Home with Steve, I guess."

(51)

"Here." He walked into his office and fumbled through the desk, then tossed a vial to Jack. "It's morphine. Steve knows how to administer it."

Jack nodded and left the building, following slowly after Steve's silent figure. The cold night air touched his burning arm and shoulder like a caress. He hadn't realized how deep the pain was in the laboratory, but outside it grew worse with every step, a lancing, tearing burn that spread through his body slowly but inexorably and agonizingly.

He stumbled and barely gained his feet again. "Steve," he shouted, "Steve!" And it seemed that his voice was only a harsh whisper. Now the pain had reached his chest, enfolding him from back to front in a fierce embrace.

Steve must have heard him because the next thing he was aware of was her arm around him guiding him forward gently. "Can you make it? It's only another block." Her voice, warm and gentle, penetrated the haze of pain.

All he could do was whimper, "Oh, God, oh, God! Steve, make it stop! Make it stop . . ." It had enfolded his chest now, and was burning inward, tendrils of pain, roots of agony searching for untouched areas, spreading out to his stomach and his groin.

Somehow Steve, with Rhoda to help her, got him up the steps and into the house. The pain became a red cloud that blanketed everything, all sense and thought. He was vaguely aware of a bed and hands removing his clothes, cool hands whose touch almost took away the pain for a second.

Then there was the bite of a needle, and for a while the pain subsided and darkness edged forward. He rushed to meet it eagerly and he slept.

He woke up screaming, his entire body consumed with the agony of flaming pain, a raw pain that drove all coherence before it. "Stop it, stop it . . . oh, Christ, stop it . . ." He heard his own voice screaming.

Again the hands, but no longer cool, holding him down, and

the voices, confused and disoriented, "Pull the drapes. They'll hear him all over the city. Can't you muffle the windows? Here, give me a hand with the syringe . . ."

He slept and woke and slept again, moving in and out of darkness, fearing and dreading the moments of consciousness. In a lucid moment, a voice cut through his terror. "We haven't any morphine left."

He woke once to darkness. He had no real sense of time elapsed. Had it been a day, an hour, a week? The pain was bearable, not any less, but bearable, always with him, dulling his thoughts.

Two glowing points of light moved in the darkness, like planets, like suns in the void. Had he left the earth itself? Was he disembodied, floating in space? The rhythm of the two suns caught at him, up, then a glow of brightness, down, pause, up, down. Were they signalling to him? Was there some code in their movement?

Suddenly, suspended in space, he saw beyond the suns an incredibly vast face, translucent, filling the void, and he almost screamed before a shred of sanity took over and reduced things to their proper proportions. A face in the dark, a glowing cigarette, across the room another cigarette. Rhoda and Steve. He closed his eyes and their voices reached his ears.

"I don't know." That was Steve. "Stiener was right about one thing, the impossibility of extrapolating dosage."

"But if you can do it for other experimental drugs . . ."

"This isn't a drug, nor does it work like a drug. I just don't know how the hell it does work."

"Do you think the worst is over?"

"If he follows the pattern of the rats, it should be. They try to tear through the steel of their cages for the first week, but then it tapers off. It isn't a question of getting used to the pain. You can't get used to pain like that." The sound of a cigarette being stubbed out. "God, Rhoda, I think I've lost a dozen pounds in

(53)

the past few days. No one should see a man go through this."
She sighed. "The pain should begin to lessen now."

He carried that sentence and promise into sleep, nursing it to his bruised and frightened mind. He awoke again to eat, for the first time in a week, Steve informed him.

"I was getting ready to rig up intravenous feeding." Her face was wan and grey, her eyes harassed. "It's been one rough week."

Through dry, cracked lips he said, "Thanks Steve, for everything."

She grinned at that. "Look who's thanking who. I'm just glad you're alive. I couldn't for the life of me figure out what we'd do with the body. Now you'd better get to sleep again."

He reached up and put his hand on her arm. "Did it work?"

She looked at him curiously. "I don't know. Stiener was right about one thing. We had no real control."

"Have you seen him?"

"He's been here every day. He examined you thoroughly to check out your story. He also guessed that your two months was an absolute maximum," she finished drily.

"But has there been any change?"

"It's too soon to tell. We'll need another week or so."

He closed his eyes. "Is Stiener still angry?"

"More than ever. We're through, he and I, but that doesn't stop his interest in you."

He fell asleep on that.

During the next day he slowly came out of his drugged half-sleep. He ate ravenously once out of bed, and he prowled the house restlessly. The burning pain had left as quickly as it had come. He had lost a lot of weight and his clothes when he tried them on hung shapelessly in spite of Rhoda's efforts at taking them in.

"I'm just not a tailor," she said finally, handing his jacket back. "I think I did pretty well on the pants, but the jacket's beyond me."

"The pants are fine," he agreed.

"Except that your side pockets are in back of you," Steve added. "Why don't we take you down to a clothing store?"

He shook his head. "I've decided to fly home in a day or so. I can get along with these until then."

Steve raised an eyebrow. "Stiener won't like your going. You are, after all, his only human experiment."

"I thought he washed his hands of us."

"Of me, yes. He won't let me near the lab, and I'm going to have to start thinking of work again. Oh, he still likes me as a person—we have something pretty good going." She hesitated. "But as a researcher, I'm finished. He won't give me even a lukewarm recommendation. But that has nothing to do with you. He's still interested in you."

"Could you use me as a lever to make him hire you back?"

"Not a chance. That's a very stubborn young man. But what I was thinking of . . ." She hesitated. "Albert Einstein Medical Center made me a very decent offer before this all came up, and there won't be any question of references now. They know my work——if I wanted to relocate in New York."

He looked beyond her to where Rhoda was putting away needles and thread in an old-fashioned wooden sewing box. Her head was bent forward, her dark blond hair falling in two smooth waves on either side of her face. "You'd give up all your friends here?" he asked. "Just pull up roots like that?"

Steve snorted. "What roots? I've never gotten under the surface of this city." She walked to the window and pushed the curtains aside. "I'll hate to give up my garden, though maybe I can pot a few beauties."

Across the room Rhoda looked up, her eyes meeting Jack's briefly, a searching, questioning look, as if he was supposed to answer. He looked back in bewilderment. Abruptly Steve turned. "How about it, Rho? Could you stand a spell in old New York?"

"Albert Einstein's in the Bronx. If we could find a quiet place in Westchester . . . but I suppose nothing will satisfy you except the Village."

"Oh, come off it. I'm no beatnik. I'll settle for a place out of town. Where do you live, Jack?"

"In Manhattan. Are you serious, Steve? Are you both serious?"

"That I am, son."

But later, in the afternoon, he wandered out into the garden and found Rhoda leaning against one of the twisted, outlandish trees. She rubbed her face guiltily as he came up, but traces of tears remained on her cheeks and her pale eyes were reddened.

"I have to fight the impulse to shout watch out," he said, coming up to her, "when I see you next to one of those trees. What monstrosities!"

She smiled, her face suddenly alive and mischievous. "I know what you mean. You expect them to reach out a branch and pull you to their trunk."

"Like overgrown Venus's-flytraps." He looked around with a shiver. "Steve hasn't monkeyed around with any of those?"

"Those?"

"You know, Venus's-flytraps?"

"Not yet." There was an awkward silence while Jack searched for something to say, to strengthen the tenuous thread he had felt between them.

"Would you really go to New York with Steve?"

"Of course. She's all I have."

"Won't you be lonely?"

"We're never really lonely. We can't be." She bit her lip and added, "Steve has been mother and father and sister to me."

"Have you known her long?"

Rhoda smiled. "It seems as if it's been all my life, but let's see, it was back in 1956. I was only fifteen then, a sad, lost child. Oh, God!" Her smile had faded and her face was drawn, her grey

(56)

eyes clouded with the shadow of frightening memory.

"It's a crazy thing," she said slowly, "but I can look back at that child as if she were no part of me, a stranger in time. I can look back at her and feel such pity, such sadness! If I could take her and hold her and comfort her, that child I once was."

"What was wrong?" Jack asked.

"I never knew my mother, Jack. She died when I was born. I'd like to say my father went to pieces afterwards, but that isn't true. He was always in pieces, a fractured man. That really was my father, the original fractured man, completely unable to function in a put-together world. He loved me and he hated me and he wished I was a boy and—loved me as a woman, not a child."

She brushed her hair back. "You must have heard the same story a dozen times. There's nothing very new in it, except that I've made a good and decent adjustment, thanks to Steve."

"How did she find you?"

Rhoda looked up at him out of those strange, wide eyes. "She heard me one day when she was passing through Albany. She heard me and got off the bus she was on and took a room and searched till she found me."

Bewildered, he said, "I don't understand. What do you mean, heard you?"

Suddenly her seriousness left her and she reached up and broke off a branch from the tree, a branch with a misshapen blossom. She touched it caressingly with her fingers. "I'm talking nonsense," she laughed.

"No, tell me about how Steve found you." He tried to recapture the mood.

She shrugged. "After my mother died, I was just kind of dragged up by an aunt and some neighbors. Sometimes my father would take off on a long drunken spree, taking me with him. No one really cared enough to stop him. He was killed like that."

Her voice fell so low Jack had to strain to hear her. "He had taken me to Albany for the weekend and we stayed at a little, run-down hotel. He was drunk most of the time, and Monday he called the office and found out he hadn't any job. He dragged me out of the hotel. He was taking me somewhere, to some relative, and then he suddenly saw someone he thought he knew, a man who owed him money. At least that's what he told me, pushing me back on the sidewalk. The whole thing is so damned clear . . . how I hate this total recall we've all got."

Her fingers were tearing away at the blossom, petal by petal. "He darted across a street full of traffic and a car hit him." She closed her eyes. "He didn't stop yelling, even when the ambulance came, and he was yelling when they took him away, and the man at the ambulance said he was dead, but I heard him yelling."

She looked up at Jack. "I heard him inside me, in my mind, as the ambulance pulled away, and I knew he wasn't dead yet, only his body was dead, but his mind was still alive, prisoned in that dead body and slowly screaming itself into death . . . Do you understand?"

For one moment he thought he did and shuddered, and then he reached out and took her hand. "I'm sorry, Rhoda, sorry . . ."

"But it wasn't I. It was a child who lived thirteen years ago." He felt her hand shake. "Steve found me after three days, three days with no food and no home, no one to go to, no money . . . God, how terrified I was, how alone. Fifteen years old! But she found me in a crowd, and just reached in and lifted me out of myself. *I am with you,* she said, *you are never alone while I am with you.* It was like light after an endless night. She was the first one."

Confused he said, "You mean she helped you somehow, knew you were alone."

"Somehow." Rhoda laughed, her eyes wet with tears and she

(58)

pulled away. "Yes, somehow. She took my hand without ever touching me or seeing me." At his puzzled expression she shook her head. "No, of course you can't understand. None of you men can." She wiped her eyes with her sleeve and looked around the garden. "It's chilly and I've talked too damned much and said a lot of nonsense. Come on in and I'll make you some tea. Steve should be home soon."

Afterwards he tried to reconstruct the conversation, to remember how much was real and how much a part of the effect of the DNA. He had followed her into the house and afterwards, sitting with the tea in front of them, she asked, "Are you afraid to die?"

He considered that. "I am, very much afraid, and part of it is that I'm just beginning to realize how little I've lived. I've been in a sort of suspended animation most of my life. Maybe all of us are like that, but it's been even more so for me. The day after I found out about this cancer I looked around my room and really saw it for the first time. I saw how little of me there was in it, how little of my life."

"What do you mean?"

"It was so barren and empty . . . Maybe I don't mean how little of me there was, but how little there was of me, how little there was to my life, how little meaning. I've never been able to feel, Rhoda, to really feel either love or hate, and until this happened, not even fear. Maybe feeling fear woke me up. Maybe that's why death is so terrifying now, to have to die before we feel, before we really live, to die like that is to be doubly dead. What I'm trying to say is that nothing that's happened to me before this meant much—I just never gave a damn about anything.

"I didn't even have any friends. There were Clifford and Anna."

"Anna?"

"A—a woman I've known for years." Anna, someone to call

(59)

once a week, to drink with and to sleep with, and you didn't call a woman like that a prostitute. You sent her presents on a regular basis, clothes, jewelry—but you gave her as little of your time as you could.

"And Clifford."

"Just a friend, someone to talk with." How little he knew Clifford too, for that matter.

He stood up suddenly. "What a hell of a morbid afternoon. Neither of us has said a cheerful word all day. Where did she go?"

Rhoda glanced at her watch. "Out, I guess." She started clearing away the tea things. "We both need someone else today."

"I tell you what, let's go out, you and I. We'll take in a movie."

A quick smile lit her face. "I'd like that, but are you up to it?"

"Why not. I could use some life, if I'm fit to be seen in public in these clothes."

"You look fine. Let me clean up and I'll be right with you."

It was dark out when they left the house, a crisp autumn dark and they held hands and talked easily and lightly, both filled with an infectious excitement. Almost, Jack thought, as if we were doing something wrong, kids out on a lark, a boy and a girl on a date. But in reality we are a girl and a ghost, a dead man.

Stop it, he told himself sharply. Stop it!

They settled for a bubbly musical in technicolor with dancing girls and lovely scenic views of Paris and Rome. He laughed at the right spots, but during most of the movie he watched Rhoda's profile. Later they stopped into a bar for a drink and listened to a facile jazz pianist reminisce musically about the twenties. Rhoda sang one of the songs softly in a clear light voice, and he tried one in his tone-deaf baritone, both dissolving in laughter at the attempt.

"I'm really a drummer," he said apologetically and took two knives to perform a brilliant tattoo on the tabletop.

"You're good!" Rhoda said, and the pianist grinned and called him over, handing him two drumsticks. "We keep these for cats with itchy fingers."

Rhoda joined him at the piano with their drinks and he accompanied the pianist in a few numbers, tapping with the drumsticks on the tilted piano top, the drinks loosening up his fingers and his inhibitions.

Afterwards they walked home arm in arm, laughing foolishly, pointing out the stars to each other, talking of nothing and everything.

His last night, he told himself afterwards, looking back, his last normal, sane, everyday, down-to-earth night.

Chapter Five

Stiener examined him at the laboratory the day he left, after he had taken a series of gastrointestinal X rays. "I don't know what your condition was before," he said solemnly, "but it couldn't be much worse than it is now."

"There's no change then, no remission?" He knew then how much he had hoped.

In exasperation Stiener said, "What did you expect? I told you it was experimental. Did you think I was denying you a cure? That I had a magic secret and I was keeping it from you?"

"I don't know what I thought. I took a far-out chance. What did I have to lose?"

Stiener adjusted his microscope, studying the chromosomes he had prepared from a culture of Jack's tissue. "I don't suppose I can really blame you. It's Steve I'm furious with. God help her if she ever tries to get a job in any institute where I've got any influence."

"Did the DNA have any effect?"

Stiener wiped his glasses. "It's done something to your chromosomes, but I can't for the life of me tell what. They're erratic as hell in this culture." He shook his head. "If I had to guess, I'd say it's riddled your body with even more neoplastic growth."

"A polite word for cancer."

Stiener grinned, looking suddenly like the undisciplined teen-ager he had seemed when Jack first met him. "You don't look any different."

"I don't feel any different."

"Cancer you know is the most unpredictable disease in the world."

"Are you trying to offer me some hope?"

The grin died away. "You're after the truth, aren't you? No. I can't offer even a glimmer of hope. What the hell can I say? We all die, sure, but . . . oh, hell, I wish you were staying on in Montreal."

"To keep me under observation? Or to offer me comfort?"

"Bitterness is a coward's refuge," Stiener said tartly. "Sure, to keep you under observation. And what's wrong with that? You may die . . . all right, you will die, but I may learn something from your death."

He was silent for a long time, and then he shook his head slowly. "I'm sorry. Death has come to be something of an obscure word and yet every one of us goes through it."

It was on the plane going back that he realized that there was a difference in the way he felt, no matter what Stiener had said. The pain in his gut was gone. He realized it when he tightened the safety strap and he pressed his abdomen tentatively. No, it was gone, completely gone. How long since he had felt it last? Not since the pain of the injection. Not since he had awakened at Steve's house.

But had the pain gone or was it only blocked? Did pain still exist when you could no longer feel it? Wasn't pain a sign of the cancer's progress? Hadn't Turel told him it would get worse? Did this mean the cancer was arrested, in spite of everything Stiener had said?

The flush of wild hope died down. No, Stiener and his tests, his X rays and biopsies had made it clear. If he felt no pain, it was only because his ability to feel pain was affected. Had Stiener then discovered the ultimate pain-killer for terminal cancer? That would be a laugh. Why not market it? He knew enough of the tricks of the trade to put it over. He settled back in the seat staring out the window and smiling.

The boys at the agency would like that. The agency . . . He had acted pretty stupidly about that. He'd call them up and explain, say it had been some sort of breakdown. There was no need for them to know anything about his real condition. *Breakdown* was a magic word in advertising. It implied sensitivity and overwork, the two honorable badges of the account executive.

What had Stiener said, "Bitterness is a coward's refuge." He must remember that.

He thought of Steve then and of Rhoda. They hadn't said goodbye. "We'll see you in New York in a week or two."

"Better hurry. I may not last that long."

"You'll last, you old phony," Steve had grinned. "Remember your promise."

"What promise?

"I'll remind you when you get better."

He took a cab home from the airport, enjoying the lavish fare and tip. At least he could live well for these last few days. But the apartment, once he opened the door, was unbearable. How had he lived here so long? How had he endured it? It was so empty, without color or character. Had he done that deliberately, or was it just a reflection of himself?

He remembered a story he had once read of a man who had no reflection in mirrors, who threw no shadow in sunlight, who made so little impression on the world that finally people failed to see him.

In a deeper sense he had lived like that, a colorless existence that impinged on nothing, that nothing could affect. Had it been only since Anita left? Or was it always like that? Was this what he really was, a man without a reflection?

The room with its Spartan simplicity was a symbol of his life, a life just as empty and barren. Whom could he turn to now? Whom did he know well enough to confide in, to ask for understanding? The men at work? He had not made a friend in all his years at the office, not a real friend.

Anna? She would give him the comfort of her body, but he didn't want that.

Clifford then. He smiled, a little of the tension easing out of him. Why not call him now? Clifford with his carefully shaved baldness, his immaculate clothes and eternal cigar, Clifford and Pushkin, the white cat who tolerated his master. That was what he needed. A dose of Clifford's cynical sensibility.

He dialed the number, but there was no answer. He hung up and put on a coat. He had to get out of the apartment, go anywhere, do anything that would keep him from thinking.

It was cold out with the crisp chill of a late autumn afternoon. The grey, cloudless sky had a hint of snow and Jack lifted his head at the sharp, clean scent of the air. For a brief second everything was clean and alive. How wonderful it would be to walk through the park, to feel the white afternoon light thicken and grow more translucent. He could anticipate every sound and scent of the coming evening.

(65)

Something in him drew back from the idea. He shook his head. Would every moment left be like this, alive and aware, each day increasing in intensity, making what he was losing more and more precious as time ran out?

He had to cloud his senses, dull what he felt in some way. He found a bar near Lexington Avenue. Liquor could at least take the edge off reality. Inside he sat at the bar and ordered a Martini, savoring the aromatic twist of lemon, the cold, biting gin and the breath of vermouth. He sipped it, listening to a variety show on the TV screen, ignoring the few customers around him.

Afterwards he left the bar and walked for a while, but he couldn't stand the outdoors and he stopped into another bar for another drink. He hadn't eaten since breakfast on the plane and he knew it was foolish to drink like this on an empty stomach, or was it so foolish? At least he would feel it more quickly, and as for the stomach, was he afraid of damaging this body so close to death?

"I am really going to get drunk," he told the bartender, "like I've never been drunk before. Just keep them coming at reasonable intervals." He took out his wallet and peeled off two 10-dollar bills. "This will do for a start."

The bartender smoothed the black cummerbund over his ample stomach and shook his head regretfully. "You know I won't serve you that many drinks. You get drunk so I can see it, and I gotta stop serving."

He looked around the dim room, a quiet, soothing place in spite of its red plush walls and garish bead curtains. The corners of the room were filled with comfortable shadows; through the multicolored beads the lights of the street filtered in in distorted shapes and colors. This is what his apartment should have been, he realized vaguely, something of a refuge and a shelter. He turned back to the bartender.

"Drunk enough for you to see." He lifted his finger. "That's the rub. What can you see in a place this dark?"

Unexpectedly a voice spoke up from the stool next to his, a hoarse but not unpleasant woman's voice. "We'll fox him. I'll buy your drinks, and you buy mine."

Jack turned and smiled, acknowledging the joke. She was a woman on the long edge of forty. Her face, even in the dim light, neither added to nor detracted from her years. Her hair had an unnatural blackness and was carefully arranged in a gleaming bouffant. Her eyes, matching the blackness of her hair, were outlined in heavy pencil. It was a Coptic face with the mystery of old Egypt, but a mask of a face, showing neither intelligence nor stupidity.

He would have smiled politely and turned back to his drink, but she caught him with her eyes and put one hand on his arm. "No one should drink alone on a weekday night."

"You mean it's all right on the weekend?"

"It's never all right, weekday, weekend—" She picked up her drink and stirred the ice. "You drink alone and it's the beginning of the end. Never be a lone drunk."

"What kind of a drinker are you?"

"I'm a happy drinker, a loud-mouthed drunk. I get drunk and I get happy and generous and I talk." She slanted a calculating glance at him from the dark-circled eyes. "That's the trouble with the world. People aren't happy or generous, and they don't talk enough. Nobody gives, not anymore. What did they give you for Christmas?"

"Coal in my stocking. But I'll give you a drink right now." He signalled the bartender. "Two more here."

"And I'll take it." She finished the drink she had, and when another came she lifted it cheerfully. "To your Christmas stocking—without the coal." She looked down the side of the stool and stretched out an ample, nyloned leg. "Now what will I get in mine?"

"Nothing as nice as what's in it now," he forced himself to say.

She grinned, her face suddenly losing the painted, exotic look

(67)

and coming alive. There was intelligence in her eyes now, but a calculating intelligence. "Hey, I like that. That's class."

"Class?"

She shrugged, using the gesture to let him know that pretense was dispensed with. It was a little too pat. "Oh, hell, you know what it's like when you meet a John in a bar. You break your ass being charming, and they act like a bull headed for one thing."

"You work here?" Jack asked.

"No, but I'm around a lot and Sam knows me." She signalled the bartender. "Two more, Sam, these are on me."

Sam brought the drinks and pushed her money back. "Your dough's no good here, Lil. The gentleman's buying."

Jack smiled. "That's the way it is. Lil . . . that's a nice name."

"I'm a nice girl." She considered the liquor in her glass, her face through the mask was all at once old and tired. "You're a nice guy too." She sounded almost wistful. "I can tell that right off. I know people. What's your name?"

"Jack. Drink up, Lil. This is my night to get drunk. Remember?"

"Great. That's just what I need," she said with heavy coyness. "A few more little drinkies."

But two drinks later his body rebelled. A wave of nausea hit him and as if the alcohol had released some inhibiting force, the pain in his stomach, gone since the injection, returned with brutal force. He slid off the stool and turned blindly towards the door.

"Jack?"

He shook his head and barely made the street, then, grasping a parking meter for support, he was violently sick. He hung over the curb, gasping for breath. When the fit had passed, he turned and saw Lil standing behind him. "Are you all right?"

"Yes, I . . . I swallowed wrong." He wiped his lips with his sleeves. "I'm all right now."

"No you're not all right, not at all." Decisively she took his arm. "You come with me."

He started to protest, to resist, but only a token resistance. But she was firm, and still holding his hand she tucked his arm in hers and said, "I live down here, just a block. You come along now and I'll fix some coffee. You need it."

He walked with her, telling himself he was too weak to protest and yet glad of her company. They walked along the avenue, through a light mist of rain tinted red and violet, yellow and green by the neon glow of the city. Then they turned down a sidestreet of brownstone houses with tall stone stoops.

She freed his arm to fumble for her key, and he stood there, staring at her numbly. Suddenly the street shifted into sharp clarity. "Lil . . ." he began hesitantly.

She turned smiling. "We'll be in in a minute."

"No, listen . . ." He fumbled in his pocket and drew out his wallet. She watched him silently while he took two fives and handed them to her. "Goodnight, Lil."

She grinned, taking the money and putting it in her purse. "There are all kinds of ways of kicking a girl."

"No, it's not you."

"Sure. I get the message." She turned and opened the door of the house, then slammed it behind her without a backwards glance.

He walked on slowly, uncertainly. Why hadn't he gone with her? He wanted, needed a woman now so desperately it hurt, but he had never been with a prostitute.

And Anna?

Anna was different. She had to be different. He looked at his watch. It wasn't twelve yet, and Anna would still be awake. He called her from a street-corner booth and her voice was at once warm and accepting, without reproach.

"Jack! It's been weeks. Are you all right?"

"Just fine. A little high, but just fine."

(69)

She laughed her throaty, comfortable laugh. "You saw the doctor?"

He had seen her last before he went to Turel. "He gave me a clean bill," he lied.

"Well, when am I going to see you?"

"Now? As soon as I can get a cab?"

"The place is a mess, but come on along."

A while later, looking around at the untidy room, at the litter of dirty dishes and garbage on the sink, at the unmade bed, he wondered what he was doing here, and yet he was glad he had come. As untidy as the room was, with all its dirt it was lived in, alive. He knew what he wanted from her, what she was efficiently prepared to give. And why not? He hadn't wanted more than this in all the years since Anita had left him.

They'd like that at the agency, he thought. They'd like to see him now in this apartment. Freeman, the particular one, the obsessively neat and organized man.

"You look as if you've had a bad night." She led him into the bedroom, and as he began to unknot his tie she slipped out of her housecoat. She had nothing on underneath, and he looked at her with a curious detachment, feeling desire arise with a cold, automatic reflex. Sex without feeling, without emotion. But that's what it always was with Anna.

In her thirties, with the still soft, but not fat body of youth, Anna's face was pretty, colorless without makeup. She capped it with short tight brown hair cut like a boy's.

Putting her arms around him she whispered, "What's wrong, Jack? You wanted to come." She ran her hand down his chest, unbuttoning his shirt, moving her palms over the hair of his chest. "Jack?"

Disgust and anger filled him, anger at himself, at her, at Stiener, at the whole rotten deal that had been handed to him. And yet, more than anger, there was a sudden, burning passion

(70)

that bewildered him. Even if he had wanted to resist her now, he was powerless to fight this need. But it had always been like this with Anna, and perhaps that was what he wanted, what he needed. She forced life into him.

But now his desire was born of anger and cruelty. He pulled her to him savagely, kissing her lips, her cheeks, her throat, but kissing to bruise and hurt, as if in pain and savagery there was a chance at life.

Anna responded with an intensity to match his own. Her arms pulled him close, and she moaned softly, wantonly. He pushed her down on the bed and kissed her brutally, the force of his lips against her teeth drawing blood, his own or hers. He could taste the salty, acrid sting of it.

He ran his hand up her side, cupping her breast cruelly, pressing the nipple between his fingers, tightening his grip as he felt her wince. He moved his hand down, over the gentle mound of her stomach, feeling the softness of her hair, searching, probing.

The violence of his desire, his sexual need and urgency seemed to boil within him, he twisted above her, pinning her arms with his hands. And then, out of the corner of his eye, he saw the apartment door open, saw a man stealthily move inside and close the door behind him.

He froze as if a bucket of ice water had been flung at him, and turned to watch the intruder move quietly towards the bedroom door.

"Jack, what is it, what's wrong?" Anna asked, and at the sound of her voice the intruder stopped.

Without thinking, Jack sprang from the bed and pulled open the door. He found himself face to face with a bulky stranger. He had a confused impression of torn blue work clothes and sandy hair, a red face and spread hands. He was aware of his own nakedness and vulnerability, and then, as he heard Anna scream, a wave of fury and fear washed through him. The frustration of aborted sexual desire combined with anger left him weak and shaken. Without thinking, he hurled himself forward, his hands outstretched.

"Don'-gimme-no-trouble . . ." It was an inarticulate mumble as the intruder met his lunge. For one second they swayed together, then Jack felt himself flung aside with brutal force. He slammed against a table, and a wave of pain lanced through his naked, defenseless body. Cursing, he staggered to his feet and lurched forward again. He had a confused impression of Anna shouting, and then the stranger hit him, a short, hard punishing blow that sent him staggering back.

He shook his head, and a feral wave of hate exploded in his brain. His lips curled back from his teeth as he leaped forward, his hands clawing, his teeth gouging, fighting, not like a man, but like an animal. The intruder gave way before his onslaught, and the man's retreat added fire to his own violence.

His reaction in that brief moment was out of all proportion. It was compounded of the days of despair, the sexual frustration and the shock of the burglar's entry. Now there was only one blazing urge within him, to tear and claw and kill, like an animal, like a wolf defending his lair.

Again he threw himself at the stranger, and the man struck back, but with a kind of desperation, wanting only to get clear, to get away. Anna had stopped screaming, and he could dimly hear her fumbling with the telephone. Then he was flung aside again, smashing painfully into the wall.

A deep growl rumbled in his throat. If he were an animal, if he were a wolf, he would kill, tear and kill! Again he growled, and abruptly dropped to all fours, his lips pulling away from his fangs, his body lengthening, thinning, his hands and feet turning to claws, his skin to silver-grey fur, his face elongating, his muzzle protruding.

The intruder's jaw dropped open, and abruptly he screamed.

(72)

Looking up from the telephone, Anna dropped it and cried out in terror, shrinking back on the bed.

For a moment the man-wolf caught the odor of fear and terror, as sharp and clear as a blow, and it evoked an answer from some dim, prehistoric abyss. His fangs bare, he leaped at the man, raking his skin and flesh with one swipe, the jacket tearing away in his jaws.

The man screamed again, stumbled to his knees and then lunged forward, fumbling for the apartment door. The man-wolf started after him, then paused as he heard Anna's voice, "No, no . . . oh, God, no!"

He turned from the door, lifting his lips from his fangs, the wolf fighting with its first taste of blood, the man struggling for sanity, for words to explain, to comfort, but only a low growl came out. Realization was like a hammerblow, sending the man part of him scrambling away in terror while the wolf part lifted its grey furry muzzle. The hated odor of fear pressed in on him, but he saw the square window and the moon beyond.

He howled once as he heard the apartment door slam, and then he leaped forward, smashing through the glass panes of the window, slipping on the iron fire escape, struggling for a footing. He found the steps and he scrambled down them, his claws tapping at the metal rungs. He leaped to the street from the last story, still hearing Anna's screams, and he raced through the alley and down the side street, a lean, grey wolf, his eyes gleaming with reflected light.

Wolf mind based on instinct and man memory struggled for domination. The wolf felt fear and a snarling antagonism at the scent of man—the man mind remembered the park and green things and drew back as footsteps hurried past.

Searching for him? Man reason said impossible; the beast knew they were after him. Back into an alley, and then a loose board, another alley and across a street in the shadows. Stick to

(73)

the shadows, man brain cried. Another street and then, lifting his muzzle, he caught the scent of growing things, the rich, musty odor of earth.

He set out with a loping run, dodging traffic as brakes squealed and a taxi driver cursed. Another block and then, with a surge of pure joy, into the park.

With the feel of earth beneath his paws, the shadow of trees around him, the last vestiges of fear slipped off and he was a wolf again—again? Slipping feral and silent through the shadows, the world of smell took shape around him, a world as solid and real as the three-dimensional one of solids.

On a high rise of rock he lifted his muzzle and howled mournfully at the moon, then slipped easily into the shadows, into the night.

He ran till the dawn, within the few square miles of Central Park, and then he stretched out in physical exhaustion in a rocky cleft and slept—and woke at noon, a man again, a naked, shivering man.

Chapter Six

He closed his eyes, then opened them again, wincing at the sunlight that burned out of the cold blue sky. He was lying naked in a cleft of rock, leafless branches and trees half screening him from the sight of any passerby.

Painfully, he pulled himself to a sitting position, staring about him in bewilderment and growing fear. Last night was clear in his mind, every moment of it, the wild race through the park, the mournful howling at the moon, the fantastic world of scent that had opened to him as a wolf.

As a wolf! He had been a wolf. It was no hallucination, no dream—or was this the dream? How often had he dreamed of wandering naked through crowded streets, hiding in doorways, feeling a growing anxiety? But those had been dreams, and this was real, terribly real.

He looked down at his body, and slowly the realization of his predicament sank home. Somehow he was naked, in Central Park—it was Central Park, he could see the buildings lining it, east and west. How had he gotten here? Why?

He leaned forward and hugged his knees. Never mind that. How was he to get out? He couldn't walk along the paths in broad daylight. Wait till dark? And then what? Even if somehow, he could slink through the park unnoticed, there was still the city. At any hour of the night it was alive. He'd never make it to his apartment unnoticed.

He got to his feet slowly, raising his head above the cleft of rock that protected him. He was on top of a small hill about twenty-five feet high. The grey rock sloped down to a little stream, and across it a tangled wood of bare trees and then a winding path with benches.

There were men on the benches, getting the last bit of autumn sunlight, their backs to him. Some were in their shirt sleeves or jackets; most had thrown their coats over the benches. One man had stretched out the length of the bench, his jacket balled up for a pillow.

In the other direction the rock fell away, some fifty feet down to a lake filled with rowboats, to an iron bridge and beyond the bridge the green angel of the Bethesda Fountain raised her arm in benediction. From the fountain the sound of children laughing drifted to him on the cold air.

Desperately he turned back to the path and the benches. Think! Dear God, what could he do? There had to be something, someone who could help him. Christ, what a mess! He rubbed his eyes and sank back against the rock, fighting down the panic that filled him. Be calm. Never mind how this hap-

(76)

pened, the thing to concentrate on is how to get out of it. Who could help him?

Clifford. Of course! Clifford worked at home. He was bound to be in his studio. If he could get to a phone. He stood up and stared around wildly. Yes, there was a phone booth near the boathouse. He could call him, and Clifford would come and bring him clothing.

But he couldn't walk down to the boathouse naked. He couldn't go anywhere like this. He shivered as he became conscious of the cold, and he rubbed his arms. If he could move around, run—but he didn't dare come out of the shelter of the cleft. Even if he waited here till after dark and wasn't discovered, even if he reached the booth, how could he make a phone call with no money? Could he flash the operator, call collect? Not from a dial phone, not in the city.

His eyes came back to the sleeping man. If he could steal up behind him and grab his jacket. But his jacket was under his head. He'd wake up. Even if he didn't, what if anyone saw him stealing up to a sleeping man like this . . .

Last night, he thought with a sudden irrational surge of pride. Last night I could have taken the jacket and outrun him. I could have outrun anyone, any animal! He felt his legs tense, and he half rose on the balls of his feet. Then he dropped back in dismay. Was he crazy? The pride changed to sick shame. Christ, what had happened to him? He had run out of Anna's place naked, drunk and naked, thinking he was a wolf?

That must have been what happened. Of course! He remembered drinking, calling Anna when he was half stoned. He remembered her room, starting to make love, the intruder, and then . . .

Something had happened. Something had snapped inside him, some half-remembered animal part of his brain had taken over. My God, he thought with a sick recall, he had smashed the

(77)

window, leaped out on the fire escape with no clothes and he had run through the city like that. Poor Anna. Oh, Christ, what had she thought?

And yet the night was so clear in his memory, every detail of it. He hadn't felt drunk. No, he had felt alive, alive as he had never been before.

He looked back at the benches. On the one next to the sleeping man's, another man sat hunched forward, his head on his chest, his topcoat thrown over the back of the bench. Was he sleeping? He must be. No one could sit like that without being asleep. The two benches were isolated from the others, out of anyone's direct line of vision.

Jack made up his mind instantly and acted before he could hesitate. He lifted himself out of the rocky cleft and on silent feet raced down the rock, jumped over the stream and paused behind the bench for a tense second. The man still sat hunched forward, unmoving, snoring very softly. Quickly Jack grabbed the topcoat and ran.

Incredibly, no one had noticed him. No one moved. The man on the bench lay still. The man whose coat he had taken still slept, hunched forward.

It was a grey topcoat, shapeless enough to fit anyone, and he struggled into it as he ran, only anxious to put as much distance between himself and the bench as he could.

He turned and looked back as he reached the lake. There was no one coming after him. No one had seen him or if they had, they had ignored him. He slowed down to a walk and found himself breathing heavily, his throat raw from exertion.

The coat came down to his knees and he could button it at his throat. His bare feet and bare legs were peculiar enough, but at least he was not naked. There were men who wore shorts, he told himself, even in this weather. There were young men who went barefoot. It didn't matter as long as his body was covered.

What a difference clothes made; what security to have some

(78)

covering, some mask to crouch behind, the protected feel of a covered body.

Ahead of him he saw a police officer walking along slowly, and he felt his throat tighten. He turned and cut off the path into the woods, wincing as the twigs cut into his bare feet. The police were his only problem. Anyone else in the park, hell, in the entire city, would only stare and turn away. A policeman might ask questions. How uncovered could a man be, by law?

He thrust his hands into the pockets of the coat, and he felt coins and a handkerchief in one of them. He winced as he took out the dirty, crusted handkerchief and he flung it aside, then he reached in and brought out the coins. There were two quarters, a dime and seven pennies. Thank God for that. He could hardly believe his luck. There was still no sign of pursuit, but he had a coat and some change. Now if he could find a phone and call Clifford, ask him to bring some pants and shoes.

He began to shiver with a delayed reaction to the cold. He still wanted to believe that it was a dream, but things were too clear, too brilliant. The lake was such a startling blue, the sky so bright and gold, the sunlight danced on the water, etching each tiny ripple, and drenched the trees and paths with a cold hard light.

The grey paths, the still-green lawns, the red of a passing car, the yellow of a child's balloon, were all vivid, almost painful to his eyes.

But it was not only his eyes. All his senses were assaulted. His hearing was amazingly acute, his sense of smell keen and crisp. He heard sound, saw images, smelt odors and felt the touch of the wind, the texture of the walk under his feet, all in a rich vivid rush of impressions, almost a painful flooding of sensation.

Everything was more brilliant, he realized with a start, than it had been in years. What had happened to his senses to make him so aware? And his eyes—the years had built up some farsightedness, but that was gone now. He could see every detail of the buildings across the park, and every hair on the back of his hand when he held it up. He was aware of things too, of everything about him, an awareness that he had felt last night, racing through the moonlight.

He shivered and pushed the memory aside. Right now he had to get out of the park. If he climbed the steps behind the fountain, he could reach the 72nd Street cut-through and perhaps catch a cab. But with only 67 cents in change, barefoot and barelegged—what cab would stop for him? No. The sensible thing would be to call Clifford. There was a phone booth near the boathouse and he could make the call from there. In the meanwhile he hurried on, his hands shoved into his pockets, his skin a mass of gooseflesh under the light topcoat.

He reached the boathouse and the phone booth, but someone was in it. Shivering, he waited till he left, then hurried over and shut himself into the booth.

He started to dial and then forgot the number. He hung up, terrified that his dime wouldn't be returned, and felt a flood of relief when it was. He dialed information and got Clifford's number, dialed it and waited frantically as the phone rang again and again. He had to be home, dear God, let him be home!

He felt his body go limp with relief as the ringing stopped and Clifford said, "McNally here."

"Cliff—oh, Christ, thank God you're in!"

"I'm just about. I was on my way out for some lunch and I heard the phone—Jack? What's wrong? You sound funny."

"Oh, my God—funny!" he fought back an urge to giggle. "Cliff, listen. I need your help. Right away."

"Yeah, sure. What is it?"

"Listen, Cliff. I'm in Central Park. I'm in the phone booth in front of the boathouse. Do you know it?"

"Yes—of course. What are you doing there? Jack, have you

been drinking? At this hour?"

"Cliff, I'm half naked but I'm sober. I just stole an overcoat. I have no money, no shoes or pants, Cliff. Oh, Christ, can you get a cab and pick me up?"

There was a long silence, and then slowly, carefully, Clifford said, "You're not putting me on, Jack?"

"My God, no! Cliff, please!"

There was no mistaking the desperation in his voice. Clifford said, "I'll be there in ten minutes. Hold on."

He waited in the booth, an endless agonizing wait, desperately watching every cab as it raced past in the park road. One stopped and he started forward, but it was a woman and child.

Someone rattled the door of the phone booth and he turned, startled, to see an annoyed young lady spread her hands and shrug. "Are you finished?"

"In a minute." He picked up the phone and fished out a quarter.

She looked down at his bare legs through the glass door and shook her head. "What do you think you are, mister? Superman?"

He dropped the quarter in and dialed WE 6-1212, nodding his head at the taped weather report, talking every now and then as the girl watched suspiciously.

He was covered with sweat, in spite of the cold, when a cab slowed down in front of the boathouse and Clifford opened the door. Jack raced out of the booth and climbed into the cab, slamming the door behind him.

"Jesus—I thought you'd never get here."

"You weren't kidding. Are you naked under that coat?" Clifford asked.

He leaned forward and gave the driver his address, and then collapsed in the seat as the cab took off.

"You want to talk now, or wait?" Clifford asked, staring at him.

(81)

He started to answer, but the taxi driver, turning, interrupted. "Tell him now, mister. You can't expect me to go through a day without knowing how you got into Central Park naked."

"Okay, Buster. We'll do the routine and leave the driving to you," Clifford snapped.

The driver shrugged. "You get all kinds. I had two hippies with no shoes yesterday—but they had pants. You really naked under that coat?"

When neither of them answered, he shook his head. "Man, I'm not knocking it. We all got to get our kicks—but in Central Park."

"Knock it off," Clifford growled, but he stared at Jack uneasily.

At the apartment, Cliff paid the driver while Jack tore into the building. Cliff followed him up the stairs and stopped in front of the door where Jack was fumbling frantically with the lock.

"No key?"

He turned and spread his hands, at the thin edge of hysteria. "Cliff . . . help me!"

"You stay here. I'll get the super." He was back in few minutes with a complaining superintendent who waded through his ring of passkeys till he found the right one.

"This is a hell of a day to go barefoot, Mr. Freeman."

Jack opened the door and handed the passkeys back. "It's just a hell of a day, Andy. Thanks. I'll make it up to you at Christmas."

Andy stood there. "You got no pants either, or yuh wearin' shorts?"

Clifford walked into the kitchen and started mixing drinks while Jack unbuttoned his coat and with shaking fingers started to dress. Cliff came back with a half glass of Scotch and handed it to him. "Sit down and take this. You want to talk now?"

(82)

"My God, I never knew how wonderful a pair of pants could feel."

"Or would you like me to guess?" Clifford sat down in the armchair. "You walked in your sleep?"

Jack swirled the liquor and sipped the drink. "I don't know. Maybe I drank too much last night. Maybe that was it."

"You don't get off that easy. I've seen you pretty drunk over the years, but never half naked in Central Park."

Jack stared at him. "Half naked, hell. I woke up completely naked, curled up in the rocks by the lake, like a goddamned animal, like a wolf." He hesitated, then took a deep swallow of the Scotch. "I stole the coat from some poor guy dozing on a bench."

Clifford stared at him. "All right. Start at the beginning and let me have it."

For a long moment Jack said nothing, then he sat on a straight wooden chair and put his drink down. "I've been feeling pretty lousy for the last five months. You know, you've been after me to see a doctor."

Clifford nodded.

"Well, I saw one, and I'm a hell of a lot sicker than I thought." He touched his lips with his tongue. "I have cancer, Cliff. An incurable gastric cancer, and I have about two months, or less, to live."

Clifford's mouth fell open. "Jack! Oh, my God—"

"I've tried to face up to it, Cliff, as much as any man can face up to his own death. No, that's not true. I've done anything but face it. Maybe I went a little crazy and began grasping at straws, even experimental ones." He started to gloss over his trip to Canada, but Clifford caught him up and made him tell it in detail.

"And what about last night?" he asked when Jack had finished.

"I don't know. I had a lot to drink, self-pity, I guess, and I almost let myself be picked up by some tramp in a bar—that's

(83)

how drunk I was. I think that's important. You know how I am. If I've drunk that much, well, hell, I can make myself believe anything. It must have been the liquor. Anyway, I finally went to see Anna."

"How is she?"

"She's fine. Cliff, it's hard to tell this, about Anna."

Cliff frowned. "I know about you and Anna. I've known both of you for three years. Now what happened?"

"Anna and I—we were making love. That's the last thing I really remember before the hallucination—or whatever it was."

"What hallucination? For Christ's sake, will you tell me?"

"One minute I was with Anna . . ." He held his hands out, the palms curved upwards as if to grasp the essence of what he was saying. "We were in bed, making love, only . . . I had a feeling of wildness, of savagery . . . how can I describe it? Maybe it was the drinking, this whole business of the cancer and my own feeling of frustration over Steve and the mess she made of the DNA injections. Only I felt so savagely brutal towards Anna, Cliff. I just wasn't myself."

"I can believe that. Go on."

"Then all of a sudden I was a wolf."

"What?"

He stood up and began pacing back and forth. "I can't explain it. Maybe that's when the hallucination started. I remember leaping from the bed, and I remember Anna screaming. Then I ran down the fire escape—I smashed the window and ran down the fire escape—and then I was a wolf, Cliff, a wolf running through the streets of New York. Can you understand that?"

"No," he said flatly.

"I can't either. If it was an hallucination, then it was the most vivid one anyone ever had. I could smell everything, every odor.

(84)

That's what was so clear and brilliant, the odor. Smell was like another dimension.

"I remember smelling the park, and then I headed for it, and I ran through it all night, howling at the goddamned moon. I must have crawled into that cleft in the rock where I woke up naked."

"Let me get this straight. You left your clothes at Anna's?"

"I was naked with her in bed—and I guess I ran out of her apartment naked."

"I guess you did, old buddy." Clifford downed his drink and poured himself another. "Man! If you had been picked up, they would have thrown the book at you."

"This morning, do you know how I felt in the park? I've dreamed of being naked like that, but somehow in a dream you accept it. It worries you, but you accept it."

"Maybe you accept it. I never do. When I dream of being naked, it scares the bejesus out of me."

"Well, it scared me too, Cliff. Only I don't know which scares me most, the idea of being naked in the park, defenseless and naked, or the idea of the hallucination itself. That really scares me, Cliff. What the hell is happening to me? If I can run out into the street naked, really thinking I'm a wolf—I could smell that city all around me. Solid! I can remember it so clearly, Cliff, every odor. That couldn't have been an hallucination."

Clifford looked up at him narrowly. "What do you mean, it couldn't have been? What do you think happened? Do you think you were a wolf?"

"Don't be ridiculous—only—" He bit his lip, then burst out. "It was so real, Cliff, so real. And the part of me that was a man was like a shadow, back somewhere in my head. If I could have gone on like that, like a wolf, I would have been happy— does that make sense?"

Clifford stroked his bald head, scowling. "No, it doesn't make

(85)

sense. Look, would you see a doctor now, Jack?"

He wheeled away. "What for? What the hell is the point of a dying man seeing a doctor? What kind of a doctor, Cliff? A head man? To readjust my brain a little? I haven't got time for that. How much time do I have anyway? Maybe a month—"

Helplessly, Cliff said, "We've all got to die . . ."

"Big deal. That's a hell of a comforting thought." Jack dropped down in a chair, suddenly penitent. "I'm sorry. I've got no right putting this all on you."

"To coin a cliché, that's what friends are for. Jack, maybe this whole thing is part of the DNA treatment that this woman gave you. Maybe it works, well, like LSD, to give hallucinations. Is it like LSD? It sure sounds like it."

"They're both initials, that's all. Chemically there's no resemblance between them. What I'm afraid of, Cliff, is that the cancer is the cause, that it's metastasized to my brain and I'm in for a series of these hallucinations before—before I die. I couldn't take that kind of a death."

Abruptly Clifford stood up. "I'll tell you what you can take, a good eight hours of sleep. You get to bed and sleep this off. I want to call my answering service and see if anything came up while I was gone. I've been working on a layout for the Lessing Agency, big Madison Avenue account, not like that chintzy outfit of yours. I want to be available in case they start knocking my door down. I'll be back tonight."

Jack smiled. "Anyway, thanks, just for being available. If it happens again . . ."

"Keep your clothes on this time."

"Thanks. I'll sleep in them."

Afterwards, when Clifford had left, Jack lay in bed, shivering under the blankets. Sleep was impossible, but if he could rest, just rest and get warm again. He was asleep before he could finish the thought.

He woke at dusk with a painful, throbbing headache and a mouth like dry flannel. He stumbled to the bathroom, shaved and showered, standing for fifteen minutes under the steaming hot water.

Afterwards he made coffee and drank it with some biscuits, trying to force his mind away from what had happened last night, from this morning in the park, but it kept coming back in a frightening, confusing memory. What had happened and why? Was it the beginning of a mental breakdown, or was it the DNA as Clifford had suggested? He had been sure that there was no hallucinogenic effect to the drug, but what did he really know about it, or about cancer for that matter?

On a sudden impulse he put a call through to Steve in Canada. She could straighten him out, and it would be good to talk to her again, and to Rhoda too. He found himself smiling as he dialed the number, for the first time, it seemed, in ages. Catching the thought, he shook his head. Man's emotions were indestructible.

But after a few rings the operator cut in to tell him that the phone was disconnected and there was no forwarding number. Then Steve and Rhoda had pulled up stakes and were on their way to New York, or were already here. He would have to wait till they contacted him, or he could call Albert Einstein Medical School tomorrow. It was too late now.

He toyed with the idea of calling Stiener, but decided against it. Yet he had to talk to someone. He started to dial Clifford's number, and then hung up. Clifford had his number, and he'd call when he finished work. His most productive hours were in the afternoon, often he'd work at the drawing board till nine or ten and then break for supper and the long night.

He finished the coffee and looked at his watch. He had to get out of the apartment, walk in the street where there were people and noise. He couldn't bear the loneliness of these rooms.

(87)

And yet, downstairs, he found himself drifting towards the quiet of the park. He walked through it, westward, as the last traces of light left the sky, and then he walked uptown along Central Park West.

He remembered the sleeping man on the bench and the stolen coat. If he could return that somehow, perhaps through the police—was there a lost and found for Central Park? "I stole it, but I had to. I was naked." A simple explanation.

He grinned crookedly and fumbled in his pocket for a cigar and matches. He drew in the smoke gratefully, inhaling just enough to feel the bite in his lungs. The odor of the cigar on the cold autumn air, the clean lights of the buildings around him, and the edges of starry sky—it was a beautiful night, clear and clean and cold. Like last night. But now there was less of the vivid scent of the park and city.

He walked along slowly, puffing at the cigar, trying to fight back the edge of fear and pain. If last night had been vague and half-remembered, like a dream, it wouldn't have frightened him half as much. It was the brilliant recall of every moment of his race through the park that troubled him. No dream, no hallucination could have been that real. Then what did it mean? What had happened?

He kept walking north to the end of the park, and then he cut west again towards the drive. He ambled uptown slowly, and ahead of him the lights of the West Side Highway snaked their way up the Hudson. He stood leaning on the parapet of the drive at 160th Street, staring at the George Washington Bridge, dark against darkness, outlined in light, yellow and hard white, reflected in the water in gemlike patterns.

He had walked how far? Five or six miles and he felt no fatigue. He pressed his side and probed deep, below the ribs, but the ache that had seemed so much a part of him was gone.

Or was his perception of it gone? Did that mean the nerves were affected now? That feeling was gone? Was that why he had been able to walk so far without fatigue?

The fatigue would come. You paid for all you spent, and the payment was never easy. He gripped the stone of the parapet. This must end, this perception of life, this feeling, this identity.

"We all die," Clifford had said, but not like this, eking out your last few days. And when it became really bad, when he was bedridden, whom could he call, to whom could he turn?

He bit his lip. "I won't. By God, I'll go on my own terms. When I can get up the guts to do it, clean and quick."

Maybe tonight. Well, why not? Tonight when all was clear and clean and good. End it all on a high note. No more hallucinations; no last dying agonies.

He felt tears wet on his cold cheeks and he stirred, and then walked on till he was just under the shadow of the George Washington Bridge. To his right, a hill climbed steeply past the Columbia-Presbyterian Medical Center to Washington Heights and the entrance to the bridge. He climbed steps and zigzagged up a cobbled street and finally came out at the bridge's entrance.

He was surprised to find that there was no pedestrian toll, and he walked out on the bridge slowly, hesitantly. For a while, in the center of the span, he watched the traffic race past, then he leaned over the railing and stared below at the dark water. There was a bitterly cold wind out here, tearing across the bridge, blowing downstream towards the harbor and the lights of the boats.

He watched a brilliantly lit riverboat head towards the bridge, and he crossed his arms, feeling his muscles tense under his fingers. This was his body, flesh and blood and bone. It had never betrayed him before. Why now? Why? A fragment of poetry, learned how many years ago, passed through his mind. *Here where the world is quiet, Here, where all trouble seems Dead winds' and spent waves' riot In doubtful dreams of dreams . . .*

No, it should be *cold winds' riot.* It was his life that was dead and spent. The world about him was still alive, still filled with sound and color and feeling. It was he who dreamed the *doubtful dreams of dreams.*

Why had he thought of Swinburne now? What poem was it from? "Atalanta in Calydon"? *The hounds of spring on winter's traces.* No, that was last night. *The hound of spring.* Could you call a wolf a hound?

This was a different poem, and he racked his memory trying to identify it. "Green Grapes of Proserpine"? Suddenly it was terribly important that he know, but the title was buried in his memory. Was that at fault now? Was this another sign of degeneration? How long ago had he seen Dr. Turel? How much time had he been given? "Two months, at the outside three," Turel had said. What about the inside? A month, a week?

Suddenly he remembered the two lines so often quoted from Swinburne's poem, so overdone. *That even the weariest river Winds somewhere safe to sea.* What went before? Of course. *We thank with brief thanksgiving Whatever gods may be That no life lives forever, That dead men rise up never . . .*

He turned his back to the railing and suddenly screamed into the wind, "Oh, Christ! No, no, no!"

Let him live. He didn't welcome death. He didn't want death. There was no sense of relief, no sense of wanting to die. He wasn't tired of life. Let him have life, what little of it was left.

But why? To go from hallucination to hallucination? To hang on kicking and screaming for these last few days? Wasn't it far better to go out decently, cleanly, all at once?

He knew in that moment that he had the courage to do it now, but it must be quick before his will crumbled. Now, in one clean moment!

He kicked off his shoes and shrugged out of his coat. He heard a shout from the roadway and brakes screamed as a car pulled to a stop. Now, before he had time to reconsider or be stopped. He tore off his jacket and scrambled over the metal rail. He hesi-

(90)

tated only a second and then flung himself into space.

It's 220 feet from the top span of the George Washington Bridge to the river below, and Jack fell the first 50 feet in blackness and bitter cold. The wind tore at his face and clothes, and a sudden shock of terror filled him.

What had he done? What insanity had driven him to this? With a frightening clarity he knew he was not ready for death, not now, not yet. If he had another day, even another moment, he had to live it. He couldn't end things like this, plunging down to smash his body against the water below!

He twisted in midair and heard his own voice screaming wildly, frantically. "No, no no!" He didn't want to die. Not like this, not now.

The horror that gripped him turned to rage as the will to live burned through him. He wouldn't die. A wild, almost insane conviction filled him. He would get out of this. He would fly out of this like a bird.

His scream changed to a shriek of triumph and pain ripped through him as he felt his arms lengthen and tear the fabric of his clothes as they changed into vast, feathered pinions. Another hundred feet and his flight was arrested as half bird, half man, his face elongating into a beak, his body feathered and stretched, his clothes hanging in shreds from his massive wings and clawlike feet, he beat the night air over the darkened river.

He fell more slowly, rising, gliding, struggling to free himself from the shreds of clothes that entangled him, a joyous sense of power mixing with anxiety as he struggled in the air, searched dim and hidden birdlike instincts to capture the updraft from the river, to stay airborne.

He fought the air, beat it with his giant angel wings, tensed the bands of muscle that laced across his chest and still lost altitude, sinking lower and lower towards the icy black water.

Once he thought that he had won, and he soared upward with a shrill scream of joy, but the tangle of cloth caught at his wings, ripped the feathers from them and he fell again, fluttering over the water.

Then one trailing pinion touched the waves. He beat the air frantically, but his bulk was too great. The bird-man he had become was never designed to fly, could never do more than glide. He sank back to the water, and as his feathers were soaked, the weight of his wet clothes dragged him under.

His bird-man brain struggled for life, and his strangely chambered heart raced faster, pumping blood through his new hollow-boned body. He opened his beak to scream and the icy salt water of the Hudson filled it, burning down to his lungs.

He floundered, just below the surface, coughing and choking, kicking free of his clothes, churning the water with his wings, and again the will to live, the burning savage will to live swept through him.

Not a man, nor a bird, but only a fish could exist here, and with this conviction the feathers fell away, the arms dwindled to radiating bones, the feet fused to a tail. Inside his body the heart changed again and lungs became gills as the bird head drew back and turned blunt and smooth. With an enormous twist the last shreds of clothing were flung aside and a sleek, deadly-looking shark cut deep into the water.

As man-bird brain faded and shark mind took over, he headed instinctively seaward, following the tide to where the salt concentration became richer and more livable, outward towards the vast harbor and the ocean beyond.

Chapter Seven

CLIFFORD, back at his apartment, ate a light lunch and then sat down at his drawing board in the studio. He lived and worked at home, and with each passing year recognized his growing reluctance to leave the apartment for any reason.

"Step one on the road to becoming a complete recluse," Jack had once told him, but that was a snap analysis. He wasn't afraid of involvement with life, nor was he ignorant of it as Jack seemed to be. He had been involved, God knows. There were those crazy years in New Orleans, and then San Francisco, the stretch in Korea . . . No, it wasn't fear of involvement that narrowed his world each day. It was a vast boredom more than anything else.

(93)

Had it always been like that? Surely there had been a time when life was exciting, when he had looked forward to every day, to every experience. When had it stopped?

Surely not in New Orleans. He had led a wild, exuberant life there. Nothing was too far out, not drugs nor sex, drink nor even perversions—the original mixed-up kid, but he had lived. And he had lived in San Francisco too, painted the way he wanted to paint.

Where then had it changed? In Korea, where he had learned that no perversion of his own could match the perverse way of war? Not really. He had come back still alive, and yet life had seemed worthless. His old friends, his old work—none of it added up. He had withdrawn from involvement with life after Sarah's attempt at suicide. He brushed the memory of that from his mind. Get back to Jack. Jack had never really been involved with life.

Clifford "buttered" the back of a sheet of repro proofs with rubber cement and then capped the can, unconsciously spreading his nostrils at the sharp odor of the thinner. With his razor in hand he stared around at the white, clean walls of the studio.

The rest of the apartment was papered with an olive green hand-blocked print, keyed with care to the drapes, the upholstery fabric and the rugs—a comfortable refuge, warm and lived in. Only in this room, the studio, was there a careless disregard for color or decoration of any sort. The walls were a functional white, the furniture, drawing table, chair, cabinets, shelves all picked only for utility. This room was like Jack's apartment, and it was only here that he was completely comfortable.

He cut a column of type and positioned it on the layout. But he was comfortable because he worked here, and in the work there was a surcease from all thinking. If a man could work all his waking day . . .

He sat back, thinking of Jack, idly rubbing rubber cement off the clean white of the Bristol board. He had been shaken this morning, truly shaken, first by the phone call and then by finding Jack like that in the park. But he had been even more shaken by what Jack had said about the cancer.

Yet there was so much in Jack's story that didn't make sense. Where had reality ended and hallucination started? The whole story of his trip to Montreal had an unreal ring to it. The garden and the girl with the pale eyes, even this woman Steve Douthright. Would she have given him DNA just like that, an experimental dosage of the drug? If she did, had his hallucinations started then? Was that when he had seen the garden, or had he seen it before?

Clifford frowned, trying to track down an elusive memory. Just what was DNA? What effect could it have? Hadn't there been an article about it in one of the magazines he had bought last month?

He left the studio and took the pile of magazines from the bottom shelf in the bookcase, thumbing through them till he found the one he wanted. But the article, when he found it, only mentioned DNA briefly. It was about RNA and its link to memory. It described an experiment with planaria, flatworms about $5/8$ inch long. Cut in half, they regenerated their heads or tails. They could be trained to react to certain stimuli, and the RNA extracted from trained planaria, fed to untrained planaria, caused the untrained ones to learn the same lesson more quickly than the original worms. RNA and possibly DNA as well, the article concluded, carried the answer to memory as well as to every other function of the body.

Then was RNA the same as DNA? In spite of what Jack had said, were they related to LSD? What a goddamned world of letters and numbers we were coming to. The computerized age. Break everything down to initials and take away its meaning, its good, its bad.

He looked up both DNA and RNA in the medical dictionary

and then shook his head, as confused as before. Ribonucleic acid and deoxyribonucleic acid—what did either of them mean? What was a nucleic acid anyway? He had never been strong in science.

Now he knew LSD was an hallucinogen, a drug kids used for kicks. What had made him think of it? There was no relationship between DNA and LSD. He looked at his watch and swore at the time, then he opened a can of beer and took it into the studio.

He approached the layout again and worked steadily till the late afternoon. Then he called for a messenger, packaged the mechanicals and closed the studio.

He had some frozen kidneys in the freezer and he thawed them out in a little broth for Pushkin. The cat watched him balefully from the refrigerator top, then sprang down and stalked around his dish in feigned disapproval while the meat was cooling.

"What's the matter?" Clifford frowned. "Those are damned good kidneys. You're spoiled. That's your problem."

The kidneys were good, so good their smell made him hungry. He searched the refrigerator hopefully, but it was empty. Today was his morning for shopping, but Jack had put a crimp in that. Maybe he ought to give him a ring now and have dinner with him. He wanted to get to the bottom of the whole business. But he hesitated about dinner. Was Jack—well, safe to be with? How unbalanced was he? He shrugged angrily. Hell, when a friend was in trouble you rallied round, and man, Jack was in trouble.

But Jack's phone rang unanswered and after a while Clifford gave up, relieved that he didn't have to see him. He had at least tried. He had a sandwich and coffee at the corner coffee shop, and tried to read the afternoon paper, but his thoughts kept returning to Jack and the whole problem of the cancer. What a lousy disease. And Jack had said it was incurable. Why?

Couldn't it be cut out, or treated with X ray?

He shivered, feeling an edge of fear at the thought of it. What an ugly word, cancer! He folded the paper with a sigh. It was a rotten deal, and why did it have to happen to someone like Jack, to such a decent guy?

How long had they known each other? It was over five years since they had worked together on that little magazine—what was its name, *Spectrum? Scope?* No, it was *Medical Scope.* He had done the layouts and artwork and Jack had edited it, and had done a damned fine job too. A shame it had folded.

He had asked him once, at one of those late bull sessions at his apartment, "You've got no responsibility, Jack. Why don't you get out of this advertising racket? Why don't you write? You can handle words."

Jack had turned his glass, squinting into the liquor. "I don't want to write, Cliff. Essentially I'm not a writer. I've got no drive to create. I'm an editor, a copywriter. I've got no ambition beyond that."

"But it's such a waste . . ."

"Not at all." Seriously he said, "It would only be a waste if I had the talent, if I were misusing that talent. Why do we all accept the cliché that the advertising man is a frustrated writer, that he's afraid to express his real talent or unable to. Just let him get away, off by himself, out of the rat race and he'll turn out a piece of significant writing.

"Well, I say bullshit. The advertising man is in advertising because he likes it. I like it. I like editing. That's my talent. That's my field. I've got no ambition beyond that."

"You've got no ambition, period!" It had slipped out, his tongue loosened by the drinks he had had.

But instead of taking offense, Jack had ruffled Pushkin's white fur and had grinned. "That's the heart of the matter. And if there were more ambitionless men, this would be a better society."

(97)

It wasn't just talk. After he had come to know him, he realized that Jack really felt that way. The original, noncompetitive man. And yet, it wasn't a trait he admired or approved of in Jack. He saw it as a weakness, a lack of real involvement with life.

"Someday Jack will wake up and start living," Anna had once said, "and then watch out!"

He thought of Anna and Jack and the lazy, halfhearted way their affair had been carried out. Anna, too, meant very little to Jack. "The sort of woman who's always there," he had once said, and had added gratefully, "and who never asks for anything."

How had Anna reacted to Jack's hallucination last night? How could she have let him run out of the apartment naked? Had she followed him? The sudden puzzling aspect of Jack's hallucination came back to plague him. Had Jack even been to Anna's?

On a sudden impulse he fished out a dime and called Anna from the coffee-shop phone booth. When she answered, he hardly recognized her voice. There was a tight, drawn quality to it.

"Anna? This is Clifford. Can I drop over and see you?" For some uncomfortable reason he avoided mentioning Jack.

Her voice softened. "Clifford! How nice. Yes, come now, Clifford. Have you eaten?"

"I've just finished."

"Then come for coffee. I have some nice Linsertorte left over . . ."

She welcomed him into the apartment with a warm hug, but there was a watchful, uncertain look at the back of her eyes. She bustled about, pouring the coffee and cutting the cake, talking a little too brightly, her hand shaking so as she poured that she had to steady it, smiling apologetically. He stared at the disordered room, his eyes moving to the window that gave on the fire

(98)

escape. He walked over and moved the curtain back. Had it been repaired today? Wasn't that fresh putty on the outside?

Anna set the cups and cake on the little table near the kitchenette. "It's always so good to see you, Clifford—and so seldom that you come. We can have a good talk now. With you, Clifford, I can let my hair down."

He smiled ruefully, remembering something he had once told Jack. "Women always let down their hair with me—they never let down their pants."

He sat and touching the coffee cup asked carefully, "When did you last see Jack?"

Anna paused, the coffeepot held in midair. For a moment she didn't move, but the pot trembled. Then she lowered the pot and to Clifford's horror her eyes slowly filled with tears. They spilled over and fell unchecked down her cheeks.

"Clifford, forgive me," she whispered. "I've been going out of my mind all day. I've been so upset."

"But when did you see him?"

She twisted her hands. "I haven't been well, Clifford. My arthritis has bothered me so . . ."

"What about Jack," he persisted. "When was he here last?"

"Last night he called and came to see me," she said slowly, hesitantly. "You know how it is between us?"

Clifford nodded. There was a long pause, then he said, "Go on, Anna."

"I'm a—how do you say it, an easy woman. I've never pretended otherwise. Jack is not the only man I know. But for Jack I have a very special place. I had a very special place, only . . ." Her voice trailed away.

"What happened last night?"

In bewilderment she said, "I don't know. He had a little to drink before he came here, but surely not too much. I have never seen Jack drunk, so drunk that he was not himself. Last night he was himself, at first. Clifford, I can't go on. I beg you."

"And I beg you, Anna, I must know."

She shuddered and took a large gulp of coffee. "Only how can I explain this, Clifford, without sounding mad. We were in bed and suddenly—oh, my God, my God!"

"What happened?"

The tears were running down her cheeks. "Either I went mad, Clifford, completely mad, or he changed into a wolf! An animal with fur and teeth and ears. I saw him change, saw his face grow long and flat—oh, Christ!"

He felt a cold sharp chill of fear go down his back. He forced himself to ask, "Did he smash the window and run down the fire escape?"

She stared at him. "How did you know?"

Dully he said, "Because I found him in the park this morning, naked and terrified, wearing a coat he had stolen. He thought he had imagined it, that it was an hallucination."

"If there was any hallucination, I had it too, Clifford. Jack changed. I will swear to that. Like a werewolf. He changed in front of my eyes, he became a wolf. Do you believe me?" Her voice rose as she talked, almost to a scream.

He looked at her pale, pretty face with the blank terror behind the eyes and he nodded slowly, his body shivering. "Yes, yes I believe you, only—I don't know what to think, Anna. I just don't know."

Later that night, armed with a bundle of Jack's clothes and his wallet, Clifford took a cab uptown to Jack's apartment. There was no answer when he rang and finally, his apprehension growing, he prevailed upon Andy, the superintendent, to let him in. Inside he hung up the clothes and then sat down to wait for Jack.

He must have dozed off in the armchair. When he woke with a sudden start out of troubled, dream-ridden sleep, the early grey morning light made the yellow lamp pale and sickly.

(100)

He stood up and stretched, looking unhappily down at his crumpled suit and then at his watch. Where the hell was Jack? It was after six in the morning. Where had he spent the night?

But then, what business was it of his? Did he have any right to pry and probe into another man's life like this? He shook his head. It wasn't prying. Jack had been in trouble, perhaps he still was. In the name of friendship . . .

Friendship? How far did that go? If a man wanted to stay out all night . . . He ran his tongue over his teeth and frowned at the taste. His mouth felt dry and furry, as if he had been out drinking half the night. His suit and shirt were rumpled and he felt unwashed and uncomfortable. Usually an immaculate man, he hated leaving the apartment in this condition, but he had to get home. Pushkin was waiting and he had his work to finish. Besides, if he didn't clean himself up soon . . .

He left a note for Jack, begging him to call as soon as he got in. Then he took a cab to his own apartment. He showered and shaved, dressed in clean clothes and had a light breakfast, then plunged into his work in the studio, resolutely putting aside all thought of Jack and his problem.

But later that afternoon he pushed his work aside in disgust. At first he told himself he had to get out of the studio and away from the odor of fixative and rubber cement, but he knew it was no good. He had to follow up Jack's problem somehow. Jack had called and asked him for help. He still needed help, maybe more than ever. What if last night had been a repetition of the night before, and somewhere, naked and terrified, Jack was trying to reach him?

He called the apartment again, but there was still no answer. Then, with a sudden crystallizing of impulse he called Stanton Foundation in Montreal and asked to speak to Dr. Douthright. He was put through to the laboratory and a secretary informed him that Dr. Douthright was no longer with the laboratory.

"It's most important that I get in touch with her," he said, and then, as the secretary hesitated, added, "if you could give me her home number. I'm calling from New York."

"Well, actually she's left the city," the secretary said slowly. "We have no forwarding address yet, but why don't you try Albert Einstein in the Bronx. Unofficially, I can tell you she's gone there. Try the department of microbiology at the university."

He could almost see her looking over her shoulder for Dr. Stiener, and he remembered Jack's description of the argument that had led to Steve's resignation.

A call to Albert Einstein led to a number of transfers from department to department, and finally a businesslike, matter-of-fact voice. "This is Dr. Douthright."

"Dr. Steve Douthright of Canada?"

"Dr. Stephanie Douthright." A touch of controlled impatience. "Who is this? How can I help you?"

"I want to speak to you, Dr. Douthright. I'm a very close friend of Jack Freeman, possibly his closest friend."

"Oh." There was a long pause, and then she said, slowly, "We're not settled yet. If I could meet you somewhere. The school might be awkward. What did you say your name is?"

"Clifford McNally. Will you have dinner with me tonight, you and Rhoda? Jack has told me about both of you."

"Will he be there? How is he?"

"I don't think he'll join us, and frankly I don't know how he is or where he is. That's what I want to talk to you about. I want to be here, near my phone, in case he calls. He did that once before when he was in a great deal of trouble."

"I don't understand," she said sharply. "What kind of trouble?"

"Look, I can't explain by phone. Won't you come up here? I'll send out for dinner."

She took his address and he hung up, feeling that he had done as much as he could. Now he'd stick to the phone and wait.

Chapter Eight

Where New York Harbor opens to meet the ocean, the fresh water of the Hudson has faded away, and even when the tide runs out, the water is ocean water, rich and salted.

The shark that had been a bird, and before that a man, met the full pure salt water gratefully, his gill slits opening wide to welcome it into his gills, and his lean, streamlined body awakened eagerly to the cold, the saline, the multitude of shark scents carried by the running tide, to the phosphorescent flashes of life below and the dark shadows above.

Somewhere, the man part of his brain still maintained a small area of dark consciousness, a stubborn identity that waited helplessly in the cartilaginous skull of the shark for some chance to assert itself. Somewhere, in the elasmobranch horror of shark brain, the man-self struggled towards total consciousness again and again before it gave up in despair to wait, but waiting, to still sense and know.

East, along the shores of Long Island, the shark glided through the coastal shallows, adapting his body to the water with an instinct that floated up out of a dim, abysmal, racial past. Somewhere, in the unused part of his man brain, there had lain dormant every possible instinct encountered during the infinitely distant evolutionary past, the past that stretched behind him in a multitude of life forms, back to some pre-Cambrian tidal pool where a self-replicating molecule first came into existence.

Pausing for a moment where the green turbulence of water fell back from the crashing surf, the man-shark caught a faint odor in the water that triggered a still untried reflex in his shark brain. It spelled blood, and blood spelled food, though so keen were his senses that the source of the odor was still half a mile away.

He cut through the shallows soundlessly, hugging the bottom with another new-old instinct, and he came up on a school of mackerel from below. One had been bitten, but not killed, by a larger fish, and it twisted helplessly, its spine cracked, its blood feathering out as it ebbed away in the water.

The shark swept up from the bottom, its toothed jaws, the only real bone in its body, agape. It snapped one mackerel in half, but left it dying to tear at another before the whole school vanished in a flurry of alarm. Then, together with the bleeding halves of fish, it sank down to the bottom, feeding and tearing at the pulsating bodies while the man-self gagged in disgust even as it tasted the fresh, sweet delight of the meat through the shark's taste buds.

Some instinct, again newly created or awakened, guided it to the shadowed, mottled, seaweed-covered rocks where its brown, upper body would be camouflaged and it could feed contentedly on the torn mackerel.

Afterwards it lay quiescent, digesting the meal, staring out at the flickering light and darkness, while thought processes that bore no relation to reasoned thinking drifted sluggishly through its mind.

The hidden man part of its brain, now that the shark mind lay dormant, roused itself and tried, feebly, to take possession. Once before, as a wolf, it had managed to return to manhood during sleep, but the shark's sleep was never complete. Its eyes open, it still saw the water, and it still sensed pressure changes through the delicate nerve cells along its side, it still sifted out the millions of saline odors, the ocean scents, with its amazingly acute sense of smell.

It was sleep of a kind, but not a complete sleep; it was sleep at the surface of consciousness. It woke to full awareness when the tide changed and the coastal surf waters, heavy with oxygen from their furious beating against the beach, washed back out to sea. The oxygen-rich water passed through his gills, and instantly he was alert; one twist of his body sent him away on a search for food.

He swam east and then northward, edging away from the coastal shallows, out towards the wide deep ocean as buried instincts from the dawn of the world rose within him, one by one. The man part of his brain fought to pull him back, knowing that its only chance of survival as a man lay in the coastal shallows where he could reach land if he ever changed back, but the shark part followed a newfound instinct deeper and more powerful than the buried man.

The mackeral had whetted the shark's hunger, but he knew he was after something different, something larger and tastier.

(105)

Now he picked up speed and moved in earnest, ploughing through 120 miles of ocean in a few hours, heading up towards the fogbound Labrador coast.

The sun, at midday, burned down through the water, sending him deep into the icy currents that ran below the surface. Towards evening, the sun's rays, hitting the water at a slant, turned it to a glowing red near the surface, a red that faded to ruby and maroon shadows in the depths.

He saw colors in different values, different intensities, and though his man brain tried to interpret them in terms of its experience, his shark brain saw them differently, not as color at all, but still vividly, sensually.

But clearer than the world of night was the world of smell filtering through the water and interpreted by the delicate organs of the shark brain. After dark the odors still reached him, his sense of smell more sensitive now that his sight was subdued.

Far off he became aware of the warm, mammalian scent of sea lions, and he headed towards it questingly. Then, overriding that, more powerful and pungent, he caught the dimly unpleasant odor of fuel oil and at the same time his pressure receptors registered the rhythmic throb of a boat's engine.

He nosed away uncertainly until, mixed with the faintly repellent odor of the fuel, he scented blood, fresh and rich. He shot forward, knifing through the water, suddenly careless as the blood scent triggered an automatic reflex in his shark mind.

He came up on the boat from behind and he saw the trailing chunk of meat imbedded on the silver hook trawling behind the boat. His shark mind spurred him forward while his man brain recognized the trap and cried out in silent, ineffectual protest.

He struck at the hook and half the meat came away in his jaws, then he struck again, but this time the hook caught, biting into the tender skin above the boney jaws.

Pain sent him tearing back, and then the line tightened and

(106)

he was pulled forward. He struggled and twisted and then, as the hook bit painfully into his lip, he raced forward, easing the tension, straight towards the throbbing screw of the boat.

At the last moment he dived, spiraling downward into the black, icy water, and the sudden change of angle tore the hook loose from his mouth, sending his own blood clouding outward in a maddening scent.

He raced away from it, away from the fuel oil smell and the throbbing motor, heading down and out, into the cold, soothing depths of the ocean. He swam frantically, trying to outrun the burning pain in his lip, and then, even his shark muscles exhausted, he sank down to lie quietly along the bottom, nursing his wound while the blood feathered out into the water.

Lying there motionless, with only his sides pulsating to the swell of the ocean, he was aware of a stealthy movement below him in an upthrust of rock. A vast conger eel, scenting his blood, was flowing towards him cautiously and slowly, but hungrily.

Finally, seeing no movement on the part of the wounded shark, made avaricious by the taste of blood, it slid too near, and with a quick slash the man-shark moved. His jaws cut into the eel's body, slashing down through the tough, slippery skin and tearing loose a long strip of sweet white meat.

He gulped the meat as the eel streaked away, and he darted after him, but too slowly. The long snake shape of the eel vanished into a cleft in the rock.

The edge of his appetite was blunted, and he rested again, letting the quick, prevertebrate healing process work on his torn lip, scenting out, even as he rested, the vast reaches of the ocean.

He moved out again as the morning sun began to warm the water, and he cruised lazily during the day. In the late afternoon he caught another scent, a scent that aroused and excited him strangely.

He thrust forward eagerly, tracing it to its source, and as night fell he caught up with a pack of sharks moving eastward. He fell in with them unquestioningly, and they accepted him, though he was by far the smallest. There was no question of where he should swim. He fitted naturally into place at the rear of the pack, and he felt an easing away of the troubling feeling that had been haunting him and which he now realized was solitude.

They swam aimlessly through the night, and then, towards morning, a wave of excitement swept through the pack. Far in the distance they had scented a herd of whales basking on the Atlantic's surface, lazily taking the sun on their black blubber-wrapped bodies, spouting and sounding idly as the whim moved them.

The pack of sharks swept up on them swiftly, and before the herd could alert themselves, the pack had singled out a young calf and surrounded it. In sudden terror the calf sounded, and the sharks, in a V formation, accompanied it down, through fathom after fathom of emerald-green water, and at the end of its dive they moved in, each shark in the pack launching itself at the whale, each tearing away a mouthful of warm, bleeding flesh.

The calf whale struggled upwards, the emerald water funneling behind it in a bloody froth and the sharks came after it. At the surface the whale rolled frantically, searching for the others, but the herd had taken off at the first sign of the sharks.

Once again, stung by the biting of the sharks, the whale sounded, but this time weakly, sensing that it was lost, that its lifeblood was ebbing away.

Inflamed by the scent and taste of warm-blooded mammalian flesh, the sharks closed in, the man-shark among them, tearing and stripping the meat from the still-struggling bones of the calf.

They only stopped when there were shreds of skin and bones

and entrails left, and then the pack, gorged and somnolent, but content, rode the surging bosom of the ocean. In the shark that had once been human the last traces of man drew in upon itself in horrified defense and surrendered to total unconsciousness.

Chapter Nine

Steve and Rhoda arrived at Clifford's apartment at nine that evening. After awkward introductions, Steve settled down in the leather armchair with a grateful sigh, accepted the Scotch and soda that Clifford offered and kicking off her shoes stared around the room curiously. "This is quite a layout you have." She hissed sibilantly at Pushkin, who approached with disdain, then leaped to the coffee table and sat preening himself.

Restlessly Rhoda wandered over to the upright piano painted black and gold and ran her fingers over the keyboard. "It needs tuning badly," Clifford apologized. "I used to play—God, it must be at least ten years since I've touched it." He handed

Rhoda a drink and sat down on a straight-backed chair, staring somberly at both of them.

"How do you find New York, after Montreal?"

Steve grimaced. "We found it right where it's always been. Look, let's dispense with the amenities. What about Jack? Is he coming?"

Clifford ran his hand over his bald head. "Do you like Chinese food? I've sent for some, and it ought to be here any minute. We'll talk about Jack then."

"Is he all right?" Rhoda asked.

"I don't know, just take my word for that." The doorbell rang and Clifford jumped to his feet gratefully, took the load of packages from the delivery boy, eased them onto the kitchen table and tipped him.

"Here, let me set the table." Rhoda put her drink down and began bustling between kitchen and dining area. "These dishes are lovely. Where did you ever get a cloth with such rich colors? And it doesn't clash with the rest of the room."

Steve snorted and put her feet up on the ottoman. "When you two are finished being domestic, maybe we can talk."

Clifford fingered one of the glasses. "A bachelor has a lot of time for collecting things—and not using them."

Rhoda, emptying the food into serving dishes, looked at him curiously. "Have you always been a bachelor?"

Clifford stared at her clean-featured face, shadowed by the overhead light, at her blond hair drawn back in a severe knot and her light grey eyes, so pale they had hardly any color at all. He remembered Jack's face when he had talked about her, and he felt a sudden, inexplicable sense of yearning. "You get into a habit easily. It's not so easy to break it."

Smiling, Rhoda asked, "Have you ever tried to break it?"

Smoothing the tablecloth, Clifford didn't answer for a moment, then he glanced up, with a wry smile. "No. I can't honestly say I have. Maybe I'm just afraid of the whole idea."

(111)

Heaving herself to her feet with a grunt, Steve came to the table. "If the analytic session is over, can we eat? I'm starved, and that drink on an empty stomach didn't help any."

"I'm sorry." Clifford began serving and they ate quietly, Steve watching him speculatively from time to time, Rhoda thoughtful, not withdrawn, but seeming to consider some inward problem. Afterwards Clifford brought out a bottle of brandy and some small glasses. "Let me tell you about Jack."

"That's what we've been waiting for," Steve said drily.

"We're very good friends. I'm probably the best friend Jack has, and yet—well, months can go by without our seeing each other. I'm telling you this," he said quickly, interrupting Steve's attempt to protest, "so you'll understand how isolated Jack is, how it could be that I, his best friend, never knew that he had cancer, that he only had a month or so to live."

Rhoda looked up. "You told Steve you didn't know where he is. What did you mean?"

"I hadn't heard from Jack for over a month, and then yesterday morning he called me." Carefully Clifford told them about the call from the park, and how he had picked Jack up, half naked. He told them Jack's story, his hallucination about running through the city like a wolf.

While he talked, Steve smoked furiously, lighting one cigarette from the stub of the last, her hands restlessly moving the empty dishes and the silverware on the table.

"The only thing is," Clifford finished slowly, "I don't know how much of an hallucination it was."

"What do you mean?" Steve's eyes narrowed.

"I went to see Anna that night. She told me the same story, that Jack had turned into a wolf. She wasn't lying, I'm sure of that. But how could she have had the same hallucination?"

"How do you know she didn't?" Steve said tightly. "If Jack could have an hallucination, why couldn't she?"

"The same one? It's not very likely."

"Oh, hell! Is it any more likely than that he turned into a wolf? Maybe they were both in it together, making up some story to put you on."

"Maybe, but it would have to be a pretty elaborate put-on, and why play a joke like that on me? Don't you see, Jack's just not that kind of friend." There was an uncomfortable silence and then Clifford asked, "What kind of drug did you give Jack in Montreal?"

Steve bit her lip. For a moment she kept staring at Clifford, then abruptly her mouth tightened. "He told you. I gave him something that might have helped arrest his cancer."

Rhoda shook her head. "Tell him the truth."

Steve looked at her angrily, started to speak and then was silent. For at least a minute they sat like that, the two women staring at each other as if their very glances were a means of communication. Finally Steve cried out, "I can't!"

"Steve, it's gotten out of hand."

"What has?" Clifford asked sharply.

With her eyes still on Rhoda, Steve said, "I'll go along with that, but it's to Jack we owe an explanation."

"Then I was right." Clifford looked from one to the other while a cold edge of fear touched his spine. Something was wrong here, so wrong he could almost taste it. "What was in the drug you gave him?"

Steve pushed her chair back and stood up, her arms folded across her chest. "It was DNA. Jack knew that. Stiener was using it on rat tumors. Maybe we took a big chance using it on Jack, but he had nothing to lose, he knew it was a chance . . ." Her voice trailed away. "That's all it was."

"That's not all!" Rhoda stood up and faced Steve, her eyes glowing. Again there was that long, uncomfortable silence, and then to Clifford's bewilderment Steve suddenly put up her hands as if pushing something invisible from her.

"All right, all right!" She turned and grasped the edge of the

(113)

table, then lifted her eyes to Clifford and smiled suddenly, wanly. "I want to play a parlor game with you and Rhoda."

Frowning, Clifford asked, "What are you talking about? What the hell's going on?"

"Games, fun and games. Rhoda, go into the bathroom and shut the door."

Rhoda turned, entered the bathroom and shut the door behind her. After a moment they heard the water running. Steve, still smiling said, "She can't hear us now, not with the water running and especially if you speak softly. Tell me something, whisper it or write it out, something intimate that only you would know."

"Have you both lost your minds?"

"That's a funny choice of words. Actually we've gained them." Steve seemed suddenly excited. "No, we have a little trick, and we want you to guess how it's done, because there's only one way it could be done and we want you to find that out. Tell me something, anything at all, anything neither Rhoda nor I could possibly know."

Clifford stared at her for a moment, then said, "All right. I'll play too. I'm working on a layout for Suddler and Hennesy, a medical advertising agency. It's for a new monthly newspaper on gastrointestinal disorders. Only one man knows I'm handling it."

Steve grinned and lifted one hand in a mock salute. "I'm going out in the hall, out of the apartment. When I close the door behind me, call Rhoda out."

She slipped on her shoes, opened the hall door and stepped into the corridor outside the apartment, closing the door behind her. Clifford tested the latch, then turned to the bathroom, but before he could touch it, the door had opened and Rhoda stepped out.

"You're working on a layout for Suddler and Hennesy, a medical advertising agency. It's for a monthly newspaper on gastrointestinal disorders," she said quietly.

He shook his head admiringly. "It's a great trick. How do you do it?"

"I read Steve's mind." Rhoda stepped to the apartment door and opened it. Steve came in and shivered. "It's cold out there. Did our little demonstration convince you of anything?"

"It convinced me that parlor tricks aren't dead. What am I thinking now?"

"I can't read your mind." There was a subtle edge of contempt in Steve's voice.

"What did you want to make me believe?"

Steve kicked off her shoes again and walked into the living room, taking the bottle of brandy with her. "We did that to try to make you a bit more receptive to what I want to tell you, to try and make you believe something that sounds—well, I don't know what it sounds like. I've never been in a position to know."

Clifford came into the room slowly, frowning. Taking the brandy bottle, he poured himself a stiff drink and sat down. "All right. If we're finished with games, get on with what you have to say. Do you mind if I smoke?"

"But it wasn't a game," Rhoda cried out tensely. Then she bit her lip. "All right. I'm sorry, Steve. You tell it your way."

Clifford sat back and lit a cigar, staring at the two of them curiously. They seemed so different, so physically opposite, and yet there was something curiously similar about them, or was it just a subtle understanding? If Rhoda itched, Steve would scratch automatically, he thought.

"I will tell it my way," Steve said, "except that it's hard to know where to start. I never knew what was wrong with me till I was ten and my father died. All I knew as a child was that something was different about me, I mean physically different." She lifted her hand, palm up, and clenched the fingers. "Different not in the way I looked, but in the way I felt."

"You said physically," Clifford interrupted. He was still suspicious, afraid that some trick was being played, but Steve's face, tight and earnest, began to convince him.

"I meant physically. The difference was in a physical feeling, in an awareness of things. Look, I know this sounds as if it has nothing at all to do with Jack, but believe me, it has." She sipped at the brandy. "This is good. When I was a child I could hear things other kids couldn't, adults couldn't either. I was aware of things, almost like seeing around corners, knowing what people would say before they said it, knowing how people felt when they tried to hide it, but it was all formless, fuzzy.

"At times, falling asleep at night, I'd almost understand it, but never quite. It never was more than an uncomfortable impression until—until my father died."

She sat quietly for a long time, staring at her glass of brandy, her pale eyes wide and yet unseeing, reflecting the amber of the brandy. When she went on, her voice was very soft.

"My father was a big man, not only physically big, but lusty, healthy, bursting with life. Next to him my mother seemed completely colorless, but even as a kid I knew that she was the stronger of the two. For all his blustering, Dad backed down when any pressure was put on him, while my mother, for all her quiet, self-effacing ways, had a will of iron.

"Now how did I get off on my mother? It was Dad I was talking about. I wanted to point out how strong and healthy he was. Then one summer afternoon he came home from work looking white and all wrung out. It was one of those ominous, threatening summer afternoons, and I had been all keyed up before he came. I put it down to the weather, but now I know better. Mom took one look at Dad and ran to him. I remember him climbing the porch steps, his shirt wet with sweat, his collar open and his jacket in one hand.

"He caught Mom's hand and shook his head the way a cornered bull shakes it. 'I'm sick, Helen. I've felt lousy all day.' I remember him saying that, then he looked at me, puzzled and frightened.

"The feeling of uneasiness in me seemed to coalesce into one icy core of dread, and then my father screamed and fell to his knees and then forward on his face. Mom screamed too, and suddenly it was as if a door in my head burst open. I could hear my father, not his voice, but in my head. I could hear him crying, *Oh, God, what's happening? It's all dark. I can't see. Helen, help me. No, no . . . please, no. I can't stand the pain!*"

Steve was silent, chewing her lip, and Clifford, watching her, shivered. Then she shook her head. "I knew the pain he was feeling. It almost ripped me apart, for I shared every second of it, and then it was over and his voice was gone. But he hadn't said a word from the moment he fell, not a spoken word. Do you understand? I felt what he said in my brain. I heard his thoughts.

"He died of a dissecting aneurism, and I know now that's one of the most intense pains a man can feel, and I, just ten, felt it with him.

"After that it was as if some curtain had been ripped from my mind. I could tell that it was open, ready for reception, but there was no one there, no one to talk to me on the level of the mind—no one to think at me.

"I think I could have been made to hear thoughts all along if someone had ever tried to reach me. How my father broke through at that last moment I don't know, except that he was my father and there was a link between us, so strong . . ."

Steve shook her head, wondering even now, after all the years. "I went for years after that listening, always listening and never hearing. It was a kind of hell."

"If you didn't hear," Clifford cut in, "how could you know? I mean, how could you know you could hear?"

She nodded. "I knew, that's all. The fuzziness was gone, and there was another sense in my mind. I don't know where the receptor for it was, perhaps in my pineal gland, that archaic third

(117)

eye we all have. I've thought a lot about it, and I once had an arteriogram of my skull taken. It hurt like hell, but I wanted to see if there was anything structurally wrong. That was when I was at the Palo Alto research center. All it showed was an abnormally large pineal gland. Maybe that's it. I don't know. All I know was that I had some new sense and I couldn't use it. Like having a radio when there's no transmitter around. I was blind in one area, and lonely, lonely in a vague and formless way—perhaps yearning is a better word than lonely.

"My mother died when I was in my teens, and I had enough insurance money for college, and then with scholarships and teaching assignments I drifted into the academic life."

She filled her glass with brandy and looked up at Clifford. In the artificial light her eyes seemed drained of all color, but calm, immeasurably calm.

"I wanted something with all my heart and soul, but I never knew what I wanted—until I met Livia. She was in one of my classes. I was at UCLA then. She was a tiny thing, a Mexican girl, dark-skinned and black-haired and with large eyes. They should have been black to fit the rest of her stereotype, because she was a perfect stereotype of the beautiful Mexican, but they weren't. Her eyes were like mine, this colorless grey, and like Rhoda's." She nodded across the room, and Rhoda, sitting tranquilly on the couch, looked up briefly, smiling in a secret communion that left Clifford uneasily excluded.

"I was curious about Livia, but I never realized that she was like me. I only knew I was drawn to her, and I was a little afraid of myself, of my own emotions. I didn't know if the attraction was physical or not. I was a little afraid that it might be. I didn't know myself."

"Was it?" Clifford asked. "I mean, was it physical?"

She shook her head. "It was mental. Very mental. Livia still wore the veil over her mind, the veil my father's death had torn away from my mind. I might never have guessed except that

(118)

once, in the lab, her apparatus caught fire and exploded. It wasn't serious, but it was frightening and she screamed, screamed with her mouth and also with her mind—and the veil was brushed aside.

"I put out the fire, but even while I was using the extinguisher our minds were touching, exclaiming, crying out in wonder, exploring towards each other. How can I explain that to you? How can I explain the absolute, open wonder of touching someone else's mind, of knowing someone else so completely, so utterly . . . there's no reality greater than that, none!"

Clifford shook his head. "The thought of it scares me. I don't think I could stand another person being that—intimate."

"It's intimacy, yes, but it's more. It's an end to loneliness, an absolute and wonderful end to loneliness."

Rhoda spoke softly. "Do you know what loneliness is, what real loneliness is?"

"It's a state of humanity," Steve said heavily. "We write books about it, plays and poems. It permeates our civilization and everyone accepts it as a necessary condition of being human. Animals don't feel it, except in a dim, instinctive way. We understand because we can reason . . . and we must live with it."

Clifford looked around the living room, so safe and mellow now, the lamps placed properly to throw warm pools of yellow light, the carpet colors balanced against the furniture and walls, the pictures and drapes, all calculated to create a safe haven. But a haven from what? From loneliness? From emptiness? His lips curled. "I've been alone all my life, alone and lonely too I suppose. What man isn't?"

"But you don't know the extent of that loneliness unless you can experience what we feel," Rhoda said. "You never know how alone you've been unless you meet someone on this level, on the level of the mind."

"Or until you lose someone on the same level," Steve added.

"Livia and I lived together. Oh, we weren't lesbians. Neither of us were. Truthfully, I don't suppose we were properly hetero-sexual either. The thought of physical closeness with a man without this mental closeness—well, it just wasn't possible."

"What happened?" Clifford, caught completely by the story, still felt an uncomfortable urge to change the subject.

Steve lifted her empty glass and turned it upside down. "Livia died. Pneumonia. There never was much strength in her." She grimaced. "That's when I almost cracked up. Christ, I knew what it was to be alone, completely, absolutely alone."

She looked down at her hands. "I stuck it out at UCLA for a month after her death, and then I took off. I had sense enough to leave most of my savings in the bank and carry traveler's checks, but beyond that—I began to drink too much and gen-erally go to pieces. It was being alone, so absolutely, utterly alone. Especially after having known what it was to be a part of someone else.

"Nothing seemed to matter. Nothing was really important, food, work . . . nothing." She laughed harshly. "I had my first real affair with a man, and I think that was the most terrible part of all. I found out one thing, and it's the reason for this whole business with Jack. I could never know a man physically, never go to bed with a man and have it mean anything, unless he could link his mind to mine."

"Tell me how Jack fits into all this," Clifford said.

She shook her head. "Let me finish my story first. There isn't much more to tell. I found Rhoda a year after Livia died. It was a hell of a year, but somehow I had pulled myself out of the rut I was in. I'm telling you all this so you'll understand why I had to do what I did. I was passing through Albany when I heard her scream, mentally scream."

She was quiet, her eyes turned inward, her face pained. Then she went on. "It happened to Rhoda in the same way it had happened to me, the stripping away of the veil. But her father was killed in an accident, and his mental screams tore the veil aside. I was able to reach her, to calm her. She was just a child then, just fifteen years old."

"Wait a minute. I don't understand," Clifford protested. "Are you trying to tell me that every woman can do this, whatever it is, under pressure? That she can hear mentally, like mental telepathy or whatever it is?"

"No, no. There are only a few of us, maybe a hundred in America, who are born like this, who have this built-in receptor, this clouded ability. There have probably always been women like this. Sometimes the veil is never lifted and they go through life a little different and not understanding that difference. Maybe a bit more psychic. Then some stress or trauma causes the veil to be lifted, and unless they find someone else, they must face this endless loneliness."

She shuddered. "We learned how to find others, even when the veil was still there, when they were still unawakened. We learned to spot them easily. Wherever we went we would build up a little group, a community of women who could meet on this level."

"Only women?"

"Only women. Only grey-eyed women." She looked up at him, her eyes wide, her face peculiarly young and defenseless.

After a while she sighed and went on. "I did some work one summer for a Dr. Cecil Jacobson at the George Washington University school of medicine and I became very involved with genetics and chromosome counts. That's when I began to understand what this is, this freak talent of ours."

"What is it?"

"A mutation, but a recessive mutation on the X chromosome. That's why it happens to women, why we've never found a man with it. For all we know women may have been mutating like this for thousands of years."

Clifford stared at her in bewilderment. "If that were so, then

(121)

by now every woman would be—telepathic."

Steve shook her head impatiently. "I don't know how much you understand about genetics. It's a recessive gene. That means it takes two, one on each X chromosome to have an effect. A woman has to get one gene from her mother and one from her father. That doesn't happen often."

"And a single gene has no effect?" He seemed hypnotized by her intensity, accepting what his mind told him was absolute nonsense.

"Perhaps it has some effect," Steve said slowly. "You know, a woman has two X chromosomes. A man has an X chromosome and its mate is called the Y. It's too short to match up with the X all along its length. Part of it matches." She chuckled harshly. "You men were shortchanged there. Anyway, my father must have had one mutant gene on his X chromosome. Maybe that's why, under the terrible stress of his death, I could hear him mentally." She was quiet for a long moment. When she went on, her voice was lower, tighter.

"Not many men have that single gene. When they do, we can usually sense it, a sort of vague, mental awareness. They're also —how can I say it? Incomplete. They can never be complete as we are, but they're still not like other men. They know something is missing, and that knowledge can play hell with their entire lives."

Clifford fought back a growing annoyance. There was a little too much arrogance in her attitude. "I don't understand why it hasn't spread out if it's been around for such a long time—this mind-reading trick." He chose the word *trick* deliberately, a way of hitting back at her, but it was Rhoda who flinched.

Steve frowned and stood up, pacing the room uncomfortably. "Without a man carrying the mutant gene on his Y chromosome, where it could match our X—there are such recessives carried on the Y chromosome, you know—without such a man, the trait can't become part of humanity. Women who have it, women like us, are reluctant to marry once we've been awakened." She looked at him challengingly. "A lesbian relationship is more rewarding, even if we're sexually normal. But I don't think a man could understand that."

"No, I don't think we could."

She shrugged his interruption aside. "Even if we do marry, we can only offer one X chromosome with a mutant gene to our children. Most of us don't marry, and there isn't much chance of the frequency of the gene increasing. But if one man, only one, appeared with this same mutation on his Y chromosome, everything would change. It would spread throughout the world without mankind being aware of it. I don't know how long it would take, how many generations . . ." She turned to face him, her eyes gleaming. "That's the man of tomorrow, the next step forward in evolution."

"Why?" Clifford asked flatly.

"Why? Can you imagine wars in a telepathic species? Can you imagine poverty or want?"

Drily, Clifford said, "Easily. As long as men were still human." He shook his head. "Look, what has this all to do with Jack and what's happened to him? You tell me a wild story, and for all I know it's true. All right." He silenced her quick protest. "Let's say I accept it as truth. Where does Jack fit in?"

Rhoda, who had been silent till now, leaned forward intently. "Haven't you realized what Steve has been getting at?"

"No, I haven't. What is it all leading up to?"

"But if you accept it, you must realize what it means. We are the next step forward for mankind. What man is to the ape, we are to man."

"If he can take the step," Steve added intently. "If man can take it."

Were they both mad? He shook his head. What Steve had said carried a ring of conviction, but it was Rhoda's quiet, decisive voice that impelled him to belief. *What man is to the ape!*

"And Jack?"

Slowly Steve said, "The DNA I gave Jack was not Stiener's experimental DNA alone. It was my own as well. It's something I've spent years working on, DNA isolated from our own cell cultures, as well as DNA synthesized from the basic amino acids. What I wanted to do . . ."

She spread her hands, groping for the proper words. "What I wanted to do was rearrange Jack's basic genetic structure. Jacobson calls it genetic manipulation. The synthetic DNA should have shaken up his chromosomes. It's done so to experimental animals. Our own DNA I hoped would change the DNA in his germ cells, change his chromosomes, his genes, implant our genetic pattern over his."

"And make him what?" His voice rose. "In other words you were experimenting on Jack?"

She waved it aside with a motion of her hand and there was a ruthless edge to her voice. "I developed the technique with three other biophysicists I worked with. They were all women, all like us. All right. I experimented on Jack, but he would have died anyway, and if Stiener was right he would have lived. Perhaps he will live."

"To be a stud for your new race?"

Steve walked to the window and drew the drapes aside to stare out into the street. "Don't use the word *race* like that. We're not racists. There are Negro women among us. Indian and Chinese too. This isn't a function of race. This is above race. It's a matter of species." She turned to face him, her back to the window. "We need a man. Not physically—we need his sperm. Jack could have been that man. His X chromosome was mutant."

"What do you mean?"

"I could sense it, the uncertainty, the awareness, the incompleteness of him." She turned her palm down. "He said himself he had nothing to lose."

"Is it so bad a thing we've done?" Rhoda asked softly, leaning forward. "If it works, it will save Jack's life and give us an answer."

"If what works?" Clifford asked harshly. "Stiener's anticancer DNA or the stuff you mixed with it?"

"Either one," Steve said tightly. "If either one works, it's worth it."

"To you, perhaps." He thought of Jack crouching naked and terrified in the park. "Doesn't it matter what he has to go through, thinking he's God-knows-what kind of animal?"

Steve nodded. "Not thinking, Clifford. He is God-knows-what kind of animal. You still don't understand."

Clifford, remembering Anna's words, "He was a wolf," stared at Steve and shivered. "I won't let you go on with this, whatever you're going to do."

Instead of answering she slipped into her shoes, then walked to the closet to get their coats. It was only as they were leaving that she answered him in a cold, ruthless voice. "You can't stop us, Clifford. Believe me, you can't. I won't let you. There's just too much at stake."

Chapter Ten

THE "MARFAYAN" HAD BEEN NAMED as a compromise attempt by Tom Dickenson to pacify his wife, Martha, his daughter, Ann, and his mistress, Faye Hunter. The *Marfayan* was a 36-foot cabin cruiser, charted out of Greenport, Long Island, and if Tom had been able to raise the necessary 60 dollars she would have been out of the water a month ago, her bottom scraped and her engines rinsed with alcohol.

As it was, she was the last of a few lonely fishing boats huddled at the Port of Egypt pier near the seafood restaturant where Faye waited on tables. Tom had spent the weekend with Faye after walking out on Martha for the sixth time that year.

"It's like anything I say is automatically wrong," he told Faye. "The kid is after me for one thing and Martha for another. The only time they stop fighting with each other is when they take off after me."

Faye, hazy with fatigue, had poured a drink for Tom and groaned with relief as she slipped out of her shoes. When Tom sat down next to her on the bed she winced away. "For Christ's sake, not tonight! I've been on my feet since nine this morning. You be a good boy, Tommy, and go down to the bar and put your drinks on my tab. Coots'll take care of you. Seems to me he was asking for you tonight."

Coots, the bartender, poured Tom a stiff shot as he pointed out a table of three. "Guy by the name of Hartsdale's been asking about your boat. I think he wants to charter it, Tommy."

Holding his drink, Tom made his way to the table, his head filled with pleasant visions of the *Marfayan* hauled and scraped on the fee of one last charter. "You the party that's looking for some fishing?"

Hartsdale, a bulky man in his forties, stood up and shook hands, then waved Tom to a seat. "Meet my sister Alice, and this is Mike."

Mike, sandy-haired and handsome in a florid way, stared up with a sullen nod of recognition. "If yuh crazy enough to go fishing in weather like this, let's go and get it over with."

Alice, hardly more than a teen-ager, pretty in spite of her bleached hair and heavy makeup, put a coaxing hand on Mike's arm. "Come on, Mike, it's gonna be fun." She stared at Tom eagerly. "What can we catch now, this time of year?"

Tom shrugged. "There's plenty of striped bass still running, and out beyond Montauk some blues."

"I want a tuna," Hartsdale said. He stared at Tom out of blue, sun-bleached eyes, his black hair cut so short he seemed bald. "I want a good fight with a tuna."

Tom scratched his head and wondered how far he could

stretch the truth. The boat really needed hauling. "You might get a tuna, it's still not too late."

"You got the rig for it?"

"I sure have. The boat's all set too, right out here at the pier." If this lunatic wanted to go hunting tuna this time of year, it was okay with him. "I take seventy bucks this late in the season."

Hartsdale took a roll of bills out of his pocket and peeled off three twenties and a ten. "That's for the boat. Find me a tuna and there's thirty more."

Tom pocketed the money, nodding. "When do you want to go?"

"Now. Right now." Hartsdale pushed his chair back. "Come on Alice, Mike, let's get cracking."

"You mean now, tonight?"

"Why not? They don't bite at night? You know, fish don't sleep. You know that? Hell, night's even better than day, and who knows where we'll be tomorrow."

"Not in this dump," Mike said tightly.

Tom stood there for a moment, then shrugged. "Okay. I'll meet you out at the pier. Better get some warm clothes on. You stayin' here at the hotel?"

"Yeah." Hartsdale picked up the check. "You tend to the boat. We'll dress up."

Later, out on Peconic Bay and headed around Shelter Island towards Plum Gut, the three were silent, bundled up and watching Tom at the wheel. The lights of Greenport fell away behind them, and the clean brilliant bowl of stars moved down to meet the horizon.

"You know these waters pretty well?" Hartsdale asked as they cut around Gardiner's Island and headed towards Montauk Point.

"Like the back of my hand," Tom grinned. "I've been out on

them since I was old enough to walk, and maybe before. My daddy was a scallop fisherman in the bay."

Sobered by the cold air and dark water, Alice asked, "Is it kind of crazy to go out like this, at night?" She had brought a bottle of gin along and she cuddled it to her breast. "Do the fish still bite at night?"

"Mr. Hartsdale's right," Tom said with a grin. "Night or day, it's the same to them, only not many people like to fish after dark. But there's some good fields out there beyond Montauk," he added quickly.

"Well, you open her up." Hartsdale held up a bottle of Scotch. "With this and Alice's gin we're all prepared. Let's start stoking some heat into us."

Surprisingly, two miles out beyond Montauk, they began to pull in a huge catch of striped bass. "They're running like crazy," Tom said in surprised satisfaction.

Mike, half paralyzed with Scotch, fished groggily but methodically and Alice screamed with joy each time a fish fought at her line. Only Hartsdale seemed unsatisfied. Pacing the deck unhappily, he finally burst out, "To hell with this. I want to try for tuna."

Tom finally gave in, knowing with guilty certainty that his vague talk about tuna had been nothing but talk. There was almost no chance of getting anything larger than striped bass this late in the season. He set up the fighting chair in the rear of the boat and rigged up the heavy equipment for Hartsdale. Maybe he could hit a swordfish. If it was a fight he wanted, even a shark would do it.

He slowed down to trawling speed, and glanced back at Hartsdale uneasily. He was settled in the chair, his mouth clamped around a cigar, a grim look on his face that said Tom had better produce or else.

He shrugged. They were all loaded with liquor by now. He might as well be prepared to spend the night out here. He took a

(129)

swig of the Scotch bottle, thought regretfully of Faye and happily of the seventy bucks, and then inched the *Marfayan* up a bit while Hartsdale played the line out to about 200 feet. It was going to be a long night!

But the strike, when it came, took them all by surprise. "I've got one, I've got it!" Hartsdale screamed. "Man, it's a live one!"

Mike, pulling out of his drunken apathy, yelled, "Play him! For Christ's sake, play him, man."

Tom slowed the boat down to little more than an idle, and turned to watch Hartsdale, his rod bent almost double, playing out and reeling in, out a little, in a little more, inch by inch till the violently battling fish was almost to the stern of the boat.

"I've got it, I've got it!" Hartsdale gasped. Tom swung the light to the rear and lit up the black water, churned now to a white froth by the still-violent struggle of the fish.

"The gaff," he shouted at Mike. "Get the gaff and hook it."

Alice screamed as Mike stumbled forward with the gaff and leaned over the rear of the boat, clumsily trying to hook the threshing fish. At the third attempt, as Hartsdale with a titanic lunge pulled it clear of the water, he caught it under the gills, and while the white froth of water turned pink, he tugged and hauled the battling fish into the boat.

Hartsdale dropped the rod and unbuckling his belt sprang forward to help. With one enormous heave they had the monster over the rail and onto the deck of the boat.

"Jesus Christ, it's a shark," Tom cried out. He let go of the wheel and tore the fire axe off the side rail. "Stand clear. It can still rip the hell out of you. Let me kill it before it fastens those teeth in one of us."

Alice, huddled back against the cabin, screamed, "Throw it back. Throw it back!"

"Kill it first," Mike said heavily. The shark's blood had splashed over him and he wiped his face, staring with disgust at his blood-streaked hands.

(130)

"Man-oh-man, what a beast," Hartsdale whispered. "I caught that!"

On the deck the shark threshed frantically, the gills streaming blood where the gaff had torn them and the mouth closing and opening violently as it gasped for breath.

Then, as Tom rushed up with the axe, the long, streamlined body of the shark changed, seeming to blur like plastic before their eyes. The color changed from blue-black to light blue, then pale green and yellow and finally flesh color. The back broadened, thickened, split at the tail into two legs while below the head the body sprouted two arms.

Alice screamed with horror instead of excitement, and the three men stared unbelievingly, in a fog of bewilderment. The axe fell to the deck and Tom crossed himself automatically. Mike retreated at once into the alcoholic fog he had moved in before. He fumbled his way to the rail and started to heave over it.

Tom and Hartsdale watched the full metamorphosis, the emergence of a face, a torso, a full-grown man from the body of the shark, a naked man who scrambled to his feet to face them with wide, blank unintelligent eyes.

He was young, hardly out of his teens, perfectly built and muscled, a Greek statue of a man, ideally proportioned and featured. He stood there, staring at the men, at the boat, and then, lifting his head slowly, at the bowl of stars above.

"What the hell . . ." Tom looked down at the deck. "Did he come out of that fish? Where did he come from?" No one answered and his voice rose, "Where did he come from? Where the hell did you come from?"

The young man had backed away, and now he turned his head, listening, absorbing the words but not the meaning behind them. In his brain the fish still lingered, but fading rapidly under the imprint of the man.

But it was a new man, not the man who had plunged from the

(131)

bridge, not the man who had been first a bird and then a fish. In the frantic struggle to keep from asphyxiating, the image of a man, an air-breathing man, had taken over the fish body, but it was not the man who had turned into a fish. That man was still within him, struggling up from the depths in which he had been submerged, that man still fought for identity. This was an idealized abstraction, man as a dictionary would illustrate him.

"Who the hell are you?" Tom repeated.

When an event occurs that passes belief, the human mind finds it easier not to believe. Hartsdale weighed the possibility of a shark turning into a man and rejected it at once. Since it was impossible, it hadn't happened, and they had pulled a man aboard, a naked man out of the sea, but they had all been too drunk to know it. The mind plays strange tricks, he told himself comfortingly.

"There never was a shark," he said to Tom soberly. "We were all loaded. We pull a guy out of the water and we see a shark. For Christ's sake, throw him a coat or something."

Alice took her hands from her eyes and stared at him. "But I saw a shark."

"You think you did," he said rationally, nodding at Mike, who was still heaving over the side of the boat. "That's how loaded we were. Haven't you got any extra clothes, Dickenson?"

Tom shook himself as if shrugging off a bad dream. Maybe Hartsdale was right. He ducked into the cabin and came out with a pair of pants and a jacket. "Here." He held them out to the motionless man. "Get into these."

Hartsdale put his arm around Alice. "It's all right, sis. We fished him out of the water. He must have fallen overboard from some ship. He looks as if he's in shock."

"But the blood . . ."

"All right," he said angrily. "I hooked a shark, but we never pulled him up. This is a man."

Mike, turning his back to the rail, sank down into a squat,

holding his face in his hands. "God, I'm sick."

Tom, still holding the clothes out, said, "Take them. Put them on. Get covered."

The boy backed away till he touched the rail. He looked back at the water and there was a momentary flicker of life behind his eyes, then the blankness descended again.

"Here." Tom shoved the clothes forward. "I've got to get back to the wheel."

Hesitantly, the boy took the clothes, and Tom turned and hurried to the wheel. Without even asking Hartsdale, he checked the compass and the stars, saw the lights off Montauk, and revving up the motor headed back towards port. He switched off the cabin light, leaving the group in semidarkness. At the stern Hartsdale approached the boy gently, showing how to pull the pants on and button the jacket.

"The poor kid is shocked," he told Alice. "Who knows how long he's been in the water. But he'll snap out of it. Won't you, son?" He smiled at the boy and slowly, awkwardly, the boy smiled back.

Alice stared at him as the boat throbbed ahead, and finally she said softly, "God, he's handsome. But he scares me. There's something missing."

With the clothes on, the boy began to shiver, and Hartsdale took the bottle of Scotch and handed it to him, lifting it up first and taking a swallow to show him how.

The boy took it, imitating him, but as the liquor touched his lips, he spat it out and began to cough. He moved away apprehensively, but Hartsdale took his arm. "It's okay. It's okay. Hey, Tom, can you push it? This kid is in a bad way."

The rest of the trip was made in silence, except for the roar of the motor and the shuddering of the deck. At the Port of Egypt dock Tom secured the boat while Hartsdale helped the others off. Once on the dock the boy hesitated, staring uncertainly back at the boat and then to the water, to the wide, dark expanse

(133)

of the bay. His hand touched his chest and moved uncertainly down his body. Then he lifted it and stared at his fingers, spreading them and flexing them.

"He's still shook up," Hartsdale said confidently. "Come on, Alice. Help me get Mike back."

But Mike shook off their arms. "I can walk, damn it! Just let me get away from that—fish."

Left alone for a moment, while Tom tended to the boat, the boy followed the faint, unfamiliar tendrils of thought that wandered into his numbed brain, that probed out tentatively from the man that had cowered so long within the shark.

As a shark, his man consciousness had been half withdrawn, half forced back into the shadowy, almost unconscious fringes of sanity. There it had waited, taking no part in the savage, predatory life of the shark, but for a while it had received stimuli, impressions, sensory perceptions and it had been aware, frighteningly aware of all the days spent in the green hell of the sea.

When faced with death from hypoxia on the floor of the boat, instinct for survival had taken over and the plastic flesh had become a man again, an air-breathing creature. But it had not become a specific man. Jack's own identity was too deeply buried for that. It had become a concept of a man, a perfect model of a man borrowed from some recess of the shocked, controlling mind still cowering in the neural caverns of the skull.

Now, slowly, tentatively and fearfully, the mind came back and the empty, perfect body changed and shaped itself to the blueprint of Jack Freeman, the face aging, the hair thinning and the muscles slacking.

Awareness, consciousness, whatever constitutes the whole of the man crept back slowly. Jack, staring at his hand, first became aware of the awkward tightness of his pants. He loosened the belt buckle with a sigh of relief and then stared around him.

Memory washed back, confused and filled with terror, domi-

(134)

nated by the remembrance of tearing blood-soaked mouthfuls of flesh from the whale's side. Then the other parts of memory fell into place, his fall from the bridge, the moment as a bird, the change to a shark, the fight against the line and the gaff and finally the floundering terror of choking to death on the deck of the boat.

"Hello. Any better now?" He heard Tom's footsteps and turned, searching desperately for something to say, some rational explanation. But he was saved the trouble. Tom looked at him in the light from the bar, then glanced beyond him. "Sorry. I thought you were the other one, the kid. Did you see a kid standing here?"

"A kid?" His voice was hoarse.

"In a jacket like yours."

"Oh, yeah." He gestured vaguely. "Down the end of the dock there."

"Thanks." Tom turned and started off, then looked back curiously. Jack held his breath, turning his head so the light caught his face. Instinctively he knew that it had changed, was his own now. Tom shrugged and walked on.

He had accepted Jack as someone else. The similarity of clothes had puzzled him, but if they searched and didn't find the boy, then found him wearing the boy's clothes—what would they do?

He had to get out of here! Barefoot and still shocked, he turned and walked quickly towards the building. Then he hesitated. If he went on, into the restaurant, he would have to face the girl and the men. He would have to explain what he was doing here, why he was wearing Tom's clothes. In the bright light of the restaurant they'd be sure to notice that.

He glanced behind him and saw Tom pause to light a cigarette. The restaurant door was closed, the side of the building in darkness. Without stopping to think he ducked to the side, into

(135)

the shadows of the building, and ran lightly around it. Behind there was a low, brick wall, and beyond that a parking lot with about six cars.

If only the keys had been left in one! With his heart hammering, he slipped over the low wall and checked the cars nearest to it. The doors were all locked. One by one he tried the rest. One was open, but there were no keys in the ignition nor on the overhead visor. He had heard of jumping wires to start a stolen car, but he didn't know enough to try it.

He stood there chewing his lip uneasily. Could he go back to the restaurant? Was there any story he could tell to convince them? What would they think when they couldn't find the boy? They had seen a boy, a young man on the boat. In a little while they'd start searching for him, probably notify the police.

He started to turn away, and then on the back seat of the car he saw a pair of old, tattered sneakers. He had them in his hand and was closing the door when he heard voices raised at the front of the restaurant. This was it! They had missed him and in a moment they'd be back here searching.

With the sneakers in his hand he raced across the parking lot and jumped the low wall on the other side, landing on a patch of sandy beach. Without stopping he raced up the beach till he reached the shelter of a house on piles. He ducked under the rear and fell down into a patch of dry sand. For a moment he lay there, gulping air, then he pulled on the sneakers. They were too small, but better than nothing. There was a sense of security in having his feet protected. Each article of clothes makes me a little more of a man, he told himself, and fought down a sudden frightening urge to laugh.

Voices were raised on the beach near the restaurant and lights stabbed into the darkness for a little while, then gradually the hubbub died away. He waited on, for what was probably only half an hour, yet seemed half the night. Then he crawled out from under the house, stood up and walked away from the beach. He crossed a sandy, weed-grown lot and waded a ditch to come out on a road stretching east and west, lit to a silver sheen by the low bright yellow of the moon. Which way did he go? Which way was the city? He stood, shaking his head slowly. In fact, just where the hell was he?

Chapter Eleven

THE ROAD STRETCHED in either direction like a white ribbon, and the moon, almost full, washed all color out of the bushes and trees beside the road. A pale, lonely landscape, Jack thought, but bleached of all character, like himself.

What was he? He looked down at his body, and with his hands pushed the denim pants against his thighs. Were they firmer, more muscular than they had been? When? How long ago? He touched his face and felt his cheeks, clean-shaven and without stubble. How long had he been—like that? His mind veered away from the time spent in the ocean.

He started walking abruptly. Direction didn't matter. He'd

come to something, to someplace eventually. He began to shiver, suddenly aware of the cold, but more frighteningly aware of what had happened. Memory began to return, and with it a mounting hysteria.

He had leaped from the George Washington Bridge. He remembered every moment of the fall, and the change—but why? Why had he changed? Because he had willed it. The answer was as simple as that. That old joke, he had changed his mind partway down. He had wanted to survive, with all his heart and mind, out of fear and terror. And survival was only possible if he could fly.

Why not an airplane? he thought hysterically, and then stopped, shaking his head, fighting down a wild urge to laugh. He had changed into an awkward bird, too big and heavy to fly, but enough of a bird to break his fall, to save his life.

And then he had changed again, when drowning was inevitable, to a fish, again in order to survive, to save his life. Could he believe that? Did he dare believe it? Was he still sane?

He began to walk once more. The third change had been back to a man, and again it had been a matter of survival. All right then, there were ground rules to the game, and where there were rules there was sanity.

Sanity! But why did it have to be sane at all? Insanity was the obvious answer. He had never changed. He had imagined the whole thing in some unbalanced corner of his mind. Was he even imagining this? But why would insanity come so suddenly? The answer to that too was easy. The cancer had metastasized to his brain. It was affecting his whole concept of reality.

But he could easily prove the reality of the situation by walking back to the restaurant, by asking them, "Did you catch a shark that turned to a man?"

"Oh, my God!" he whispered, shaking his head and staring up at the moon. If this were another hallucination, he could prove nothing, could only live it out. The moon. It was almost full, but was it waxing or waning? What kind of a moon had it been the night he had raced through Central Park as a wolf? How long ago? How long had he cruised the dark waters of the Atlantic as a fish?

Again the mounting hysteria rose in him, and again he fought it down. Get to the rules, the ground rules. If he was sane, there had to be rules. Something had happened to him. He had changed again and again, from man to beast and back. That he must accept as true. But why? Why had it happened?

He plunged his hands into his pockets and hunched his shoulders against the cold. There could only be one answer to why. Because of the treatment in Montreal. He had been given DNA. What had DNA done to Stiener's rats? It had changed the rate of growth of their tumors. Could it also control man's growth? Could it also cause him to change? A fleeting memory came back, Steve looking at the cages of wild rats, looking at an empty cage. She had said something, some hint, dimly understood and now hardly remembered. He had a moment's mental image of a rat changing to a snake, sliding through the bars of the cage. Could DNA do that? Could it change life's very form?

DNA, deoxyribonucleic acid. It was the stuff chromosomes were made of. That much he knew, and chromosomes were the blueprints from which the body was built. In every microscopic cell of his body he had enough DNA to blueprint the construction of an entire man. He remembered that from an article he had once researched. But more than a man? A shark? A bird? A wolf? Was it possible that in some way he could change his body now, change at will?

He stopped on the lonely, deserted road. Let him change now, then. Into what? A horse? He was too small for that. Surely no amount of change could add weight to his body—or take it away. That was why the bird hadn't been able to fly. A deer then. As a deer he could race alongside the road and eat up the miles.

A heady exultation filled him and he closed his eyes, willing himself to change with all his strength, willing himself a deer till sweat stood out on his forehead—and he opened his eyes to find himself still a man.

He walked on slowly. What were the rules, the ground rules? Only to save his life. That of course had been the key. For some reason, when the chips were down and it was a matter of life and death, he could change, but not like this, not walking along a deserted road, not by simply willing that change.

The yellow headlights of a car behind him threw his shadow ahead of him at the same moment that he became aware of the car's noise. His first instinct was to plunge into the bushes and hide, but reason took over. Why hide? He had done nothing wrong. Even if it were the fishermen coming, what could they say? The denims he wore were like any other pair. Maybe they could be identified and maybe they couldn't, and even if they could, he had done nothing wrong. What was he guilty of? Anthropomorphism? Lycanthropy? Piscanthropy? Was there even a word for it?

He turned and faced the oncoming car, and lifted his thumb in the traditional hitchhiker's query.

The headlights picked him out, and abruptly, with a squeal of brakes, the car lurched to a stop. It was an old, badly weathered station wagon, and as Jack loped towards it, the side window was rolled sown and Tom Dickenson's head poked out.

"Hey—"

For a moment Jack hesitated, then, fighting down the urge to run, he approached the car. "Can you give me a lift?"

As he came close, Tom shook his head in disappointment. "Damn, I thought you were the kid. They're turning the place upside down for him. You might as well get in."

Jack climbed in as Tom started the car moving. His heart was racing and his hand shook. Forcing his voice to be steady he asked, "The kid you asked about on the dock?"

(141)

"Oh—that's where I saw you. Funny, I could have sworn you were the kid. Especially those clothes." He was silent for a moment. "We fished this kid out of the ocean."

Striking a casual note, Jack said, "You've got to be a little nuts to go swimming in this weather."

"Well, he was way out, maybe washed off some boat or . . . I don't know . . ." His voice trailed away. "Funny thing . . ."

"Where are you heading?" Jack asked carefully.

"Riverhead." He nodded over his shoulder. "Keep my boat in Greenport. Just took a fishing party out tonight. That's when we pulled the kid in. Thought he was a shark at first."

"A shark?" A little surprise and disbelief, but don't be too curious. Or should he be curious? Wouldn't anyone be curious as hell? "You thought he was a shark?"

Uncomfortably, Tom said. "We'd been drinking a lot. We pulled this shark up on deck, and then . . ." he hesitated and ran his tongue over his lips. "It wasn't a shark, you see. It was a kid, only . . . I could have sworn . . ." he shook his head as his voice trailed away.

"How far is Riverhead from the city?" Jack asked. This had to be Long Island. Riverhead, Greenport.

Tom looked at him curiously. "Maybe sixty, seventy miles. That where you're going?"

Now he had aroused Tom's curiosity. He searched his mind desperately for some rational explanation. "Yeah, to the city."

"How come you're out here with no car, in jeans like that?" Was there suspicion and uneasiness in Tom's voice, or just curiosity?

He mustn't hesitate. "Looking for my buddy. We were drinking together," Jack said. This would make sense to Dickenson. "He's got a crazy sense of humor, my buddy. Told me he was going to the men's room and just took off, left me stranded out here. That's his idea of being funny."

The idea appealed to Tom and he chuckled. "You gotta

(142)

admit it gets a rise. What some guys'll do for a laugh."

"Big joke!"

"Well, I can take you into Riverhead. You won't have any trouble catching a train to New York from there."

"Thanks. That's pretty decent of you."

"That's okay. It's pretty lonely on the road this time of night. Good to have someone to talk to. I got my girl back in Port of Egypt, that's near Greenport, and the boatyard gives me an excuse to spend some time there—you know how wives are."

"Yeah, sure . . ."

"My kid's just as bad. My daughter. Thirteen, and she's got a tongue like her mother." He reached across and took a pack of cigarettes from the glove compartment and handed one to Jack. "Sorry the radio's on the blink or I'd put some music on."

His voice washed over Jack, soothing and meaningless, an idle flow of chatter to relieve the tedium of the long ride to Riverhead. Riverhead, 60 or 70 miles from New York, and then what? Could he call Clifford from there? But he didn't even have a dime to call the operator and how could he impose on Clifford like that?

What then? Hitchhike into the city? What time was it anyway? They hadn't passed another car since Dickenson picked him up. Were all the roads to New York as empty as this one? Where would he ever hitch a ride?

The road angled sharply and Tom swung the car aside in an attempt to avoid a deep pothole in the road. But the hole caught the back wheel, and as the car bucked, the rear hubcap flew off with a clang.

Tom jammed on the brakes, cursing furiously. "Damn, that's the second hubcap this week. I'm going back for it."

He threw the car into reverse and backed up a few yards, then opened the door and climbed out. "It's somewhere back here."

"Need any help?"

"Yeah. If you can turn the car around and swing the headlights over here," Tom called, "I'll find it in a minute."

Jack slipped behind the wheel and moved the car forward to swing it around, and a sudden thrill shot through him. This was an answer to his problem and too good to pass up. After that first blinding thrill he acted automatically, threw the car into drive and stepped on the accelerator. Behind him he heard Tom Dickenson yell, and then he concentrated on the road, on familiarizing himself with the feel of the car. He hadn't owned a car in over ten years, but this car was more than ten years old, and he was familiar with the shift.

With his left foot he searched for the high-beam button and stepped on it, flooding the road with extra light. Then he bore down on the accelerator till the car hit 50, then 60 miles an hour.

In a few hours he could reach Manhattan and abandon the car. The police would find it, trace the license number and get in touch with Dickenson. He had caught one last glimpse of him in the rearview mirror, staring from the roadside ditch, staring unbelievingly after the car, his car.

And he stole it with no compunction at all. Abruptly he took his foot off the accelerator. Dear God, what had happened to him? Had there been changes in his mind to match the changes in his body? What had he become that he could this easily steal a man's car and abandon him at the side of the road, a man who had helped him, who had picked him up to do him a favor?

He stepped on the brake and brought the car to a halt at the side of the road and then leaned forward against the wheel, his forehead propped on his hands and his face twisted in pain. If he could cry. Oh, Lord, if he could only cry!

The horror, the panic of the last weeks rose up within him and he opened his mouth in a soundless scream of agony, then threw his head back, the cords of his neck twisted, his hands grasping the wheel.

Slowly, painfully, the terror subsided. He had been pushed

(144)

and buffeted by forces beyond his control to a point of near madness. Now he would act as he, Jack Freeman, had acted all his life, as a man was meant to act—with decency.

He turned the car around and headed back along the road. In less than half a mile his headlights picked out Tom Dickenson trudging along with the hubcap under his arm. Dickenson stopped and waved his arms wildly and Jack braked to a stop, a few feet away.

"Can you give me a lift? Some nut took my car . . ." Dickenson began, and then his mouth fell open as he recognized the car and Jack. "What the hell . . ."

Jack climbed out and stood facing Tom. "I'm sorry. I don't know what came over me."

Dickenson's fists were clenched and half-raised, his voice furious. "You'll be more than sorry. Goddamit, stealing my car and leaving me here in the middle of nowhere . . ."

"I'm sorry . . ." Helplessly, Jack spread his hands, backing away from Dickenson's fury. "I shouldn't have done it. I brought it back as soon as I realized what I did."

Dickenson stood there, glaring at him but making no move to attack him. Instead he abruptly swung into the driver's seat of the car, threw the hubcap into the rear and gripped the wheel. "I knew I was crazy to pick up a hitchhiker. Martha's told me a hundred times. She said I'd end up beaten and robbed."

"I'm not like that," Jack murmured defensively. "I didn't mean any harm. It was only that I didn't have any money, and I was scared about getting to the city. Believe me, I'm sorry."

Dickenson shrugged uncomfortably. Reaching out, he slammed the car door and Jack stepped back as he turned the car, pointing it towards Riverhead. But he didn't put it into gear. He just sat there letting the motor idle for a moment while his anger cooled and curiosity took over. There was very little mean or vengeful in Tom Dickenson, but there was an all-consuming curiosity.

"Why'd you come back?" he asked through the open window.

Jack shook his head. "I'm no thief. I told you, I don't know why I took the car, only I was scared stiff. You do funny things when you're afraid."

"Yeah." There was another long silence. Finally Dickenson raced the motor, then said, "God damn, I ought to let you walk, like I would have had to."

Jack said, "Okay. I don't blame you one bit," and he moved to the side of the road.

"Oh, for Christ's sake, get in!" Tom swung open the door on the passenger's side. "Come on, I haven't got all night."

For a while they drove in silence, then Dickenson lit another cigarette and offered one to Jack. "I still don't get it," he said finally. "Why'd you bring the car back?"

"I told you, I'm no thief."

Dickenson nodded, then looked at him slyly. "Yeah, but you stole those clothes."

Startled, Jack said, "What do you mean?"

"When I saw you out there in my headlights just now I was sure. Those are the clothes I gave the kid. How'd you get them, and where's the kid?"

Jack didn't answer and finally, without conviction, Dickenson said, "I could turn you over to the cops."

"What for?"

"What did you do to the kid?"

It was odd how flat the cigarette tasted. Jack looked at it in the darkened car and said, "There wasn't any kid. You fished me out of the water."

"Come off it. You think I don't know the difference between your face and his?"

"Did you see him that well?" Jack looked at him. "You don't always believe what you see. You thought you saw me turn from a shark to a man."

Dickenson's hands tightened on the wheel. "I thought we

(146)

pulled in a shark," he said slowly. "I was wrong." He was quiet for a moment, then added, "Okay, maybe I was wrong about the kid."

"Out there at night," Jack said slowly, "the light plays tricks."

Dickenson seized at it eagerly. "I knew I recognized those clothes. Why didn't you tell me?"

Remembering what Hartsdale had said, Jack shrugged, "I was kind of shocked. Washed overboard like that . . . I guess it's amnesia . . . I forgot everything."

Dickenson nodded wisely. "Maybe that explains your stealing the car. What about that story you told me?"

"I made it up. I didn't remember what boat I was on or anything. Or how I got there." He chewed his lip. "I know everything else," he added. "Who I am. Where I live . . ."

Dickenson looked at him uneasily and started to say something, but a traffic light ahead caught his eye. "Hey, we're at Riverhead already. I'll drop you at the railroad station. Okay?"

"Sure, and thanks again."

"That's okay."

He turned off the main highway and cut through the deserted town to the railway depot. When Jack climbed out, however, Dickenson came after him. "Hey, how'll you get to the city?"

Jack shook his head. "I don't know. If I could call New York, I have a friend there who'll help me."

"Here." Dickenson dug into his pocket and held out a five-dollar bill. "This'll get you to New York and buy you a cup of coffee till the train comes."

Jack took the bill hesitantly. "I don't know how to thank you. Where can I send it to pay you back?"

"That'll be a good thing. I can use it. Just send it to Tom Dickenson, Riverhead. That'll do it. Take care now."

He climbed into the car and drove off and Jack stood there, holding the five and unexpectedly feeling his eyes fill.

There was a milk train out of Riverhead at 3 A.M., due to arrive in Manhattan at 6. That left plenty of time for a cup of coffee at the all-night diner across the street from the station, but when Jack tried to eat a sandwich with his coffee, he had a sudden vivid recollection of his last meal, of the pack of sharks spiralling up to tear slabs of meat from the struggling whale calf, and his throat tightened in disgust.

In the train he sat in an almost empty car, huddled in the corner of a wide seat. Sleep was impossible, and yet his body was so physically tired that every motion was agony.

His mind raced frantically back over the past days, remembering every event with sudden, crystal clarity. He had never had total recall, and often names and faces had to be dredged out of the past painfully. Now everything leaped into startling awareness in his mind, every taste and sound, the incredible sense of smell that had guided him through the water, and another sense that even now he could hardly understand, an awareness of motion, no matter how far away, an awareness built into unknown receptors in the shark's body.

Granted he had changed from man to wolf to man, from man to bird to shark, each time to save his life. How had he known how to change? Wanting to change was not enough, he was sure of that. But given the ability to change, in some unknown way, how had he known each life form that well? He, as a man, knew of a shark only as a curious and frightening fish. There were things about sharks he was only vaguely aware of, their shape, their lack of bones, their skin—did they have skin or scales?

Not really knowing this, not ever having known it, how had he been able to change his body, to simulate a shark so perfectly even to duplicating those incredible receptors for motion sense?

He shook his head in bewilderment and in the dark mirror of the train's window his reflection shook its head back at him. He stared at the reflection, seeing himself for the first time since the change, but darkly in the black mirror of the window, distorted

(148)

and only half real, parts highlighted out of proportion and other parts fading into blackness, unreal and vague. From an old nursery rhyme he remembered the lament of a woman whose skirts had been cut off by a robber. "This is none of I!" He repeated it softly.

Abruptly he stood up and hurried back through the train to the men's room. He had to see himself in a real mirror. He had to know what he was, who he was, what he had changed back into.

Inside the washroom he shut the door and, trembling, turned to face the long mirror over the sink. He could see his entire body here, down to his knees, and he stared at his face first, hungrily, searchingly.

This was the face he remembered, the face that had stared back at him over the years from his shaving mirror—or was it? The features were the same, and yet . . .

He touched his eyes and frowned. There was something wrong. What memory do we carry of ourselves? Is it the man we see in the mirror today, or the man we saw yesterday, a week ago, a year, ten years ago? There were no wrinkles around his eyes, none of the lines he knew should be there, but had never seen, never really noticed. How old was this face staring back at him? He had been in his forties. Surely this face in the mirror was hardly thirty! And his body . . .

He unbuttoned the denim jacket and stared in horror at an exquisitely muscled chest, a chest like that of an idealized museum statue. He unbuttoned his pants and dropped them, then looked at his genitals. He had gone through life circumcised, yet this body he was wearing—that was the only term for it, wearing—this perfect, sculptured body, was uncircumcised, unmarred in any way. His appendectomy scar was gone. The grey in the hair that covered his chest was gone and all the excess fat and flabbiness had disappeared. Even the skin texture was different, younger.

(149)

He buttoned himself up numbly, and shakily made his way to his seat. What had happened?

Panic began to bubble up within him, and he forced down an urge to scream. "There are ground rules," he whispered through clenched teeth. "Learn them and understand them." He had to do it to save his sanity, to save himself from screaming out in terror and pounding his fist against the seat ahead of him, to hold on to the terrified part of his brain that wanted to scuttle away into a distant corner of his skull and hide, wait it out . . .

"You changed to save your life," he whispered. "You changed in stress and terror. All right. Somewhere in your chromosomes nature has put down a blueprint of every species that man has evolved through. You know—some instinctual part of you knows, some sense you are unaware of turns to that blueprint automatically for change."

It made no sense, and yet, if it were true, it would explain what had happened. There was the blueprint of a man among all the others, not necessarily of him as a man, of the him he had developed into, but of an ideal, perfect man at the peak of maturity. He had been a perfect wolf and a perfect shark, why not a perfect man?

But what about the bird? He almost smiled as he remembered the awkward, great-winged bird beating the air in vast sweeps above the Hudson, and then the smile turned to a grimace. The bird had been far from perfect, a mistake and a ghastly one. There was still the law of conservation of mass. He had been a huge wolf, 170 pounds of wolf, and a small shark in the pack—170 pounds of shark. Some of those pounds had burned off in the long journey through the ocean, and now he was a trim, lean man of about 150.

It made sense, yet the last time he had awakened it had been as Jack Freeman. The wolf, with no effort it seemed, had turned back to the original man. Why hadn't the shark?

The answer to that was easy. A man in the ocean would have

(150)

been as bad off as a wolf in Central Park. He remembered the dim, terrifying struggle for identity in the shark's brain. When the wolf relaxed its vigil and fell asleep, the man had taken over. The shark had never really slept, never totally surrendered its consciousness.

If the wolf had stayed awake, would he still be loping through Central Park, howling at the moon?

He wet his lips and pulled the jacket up around his neck. He had been a shark too long. When conversion back to a man took place, the identity, the physical identity of Jack Freeman was lost, or temporarily forgotten. The conversion had taken place to a man, a man as a representative of the species, man, even as he had been wolf and shark.

"All right then," he told himself. "You are the ideal of a man." That was how Jack Freeman's body carried man in its tapes. That was why he had come into existence on the boat's deck with a "Greek god's" body and a blank mind, and then, later on the dock there had been another change, he had felt that, a shift back to his own face. Was that also in defense, to get out of the trouble with Hartsdale and the others, or was that a sort of shifting of gears, a little rearrangement as the tapes suddenly remembered more clearly?

And why hadn't the rest of his body changed?

He put one hand over his stomach, feeling the hard, flat muscle and he moved it down to his groin, cupping his genitals. Was he really an unblemished man who had come into being after the shark? Was he a man with his foreskin restored, his appendix restored?

Oh, Christ! He twisted in mental agony. None of it made sense, ground rules or not, DNA or not, it was all too fantastic to accept! How could he sit here like this and calmly try to spell out the processes of change? Why wasn't he screaming in shock? Or was that too part of the change?

But at Penn Station, leaving the train, he brought himself up

(151)

short and stared ahead wildly. Then what about the cancer? Had that too left him? Was he free of it? Dear God, was he free?

He ran up the platform taking the steps two at a time, and he raced out to the entrance to flag a cab. He was filled with a wild sort of exuberance. He would live now. He was sure of it, positive!

He had two dollars left from the five, enough to get home. In the cab he leaned back and closed his eyes, but he was smiling. It had to be true. It had to be!

Chapter Twelve

AFTER A SLEEPLESS NIGHT, Clifford woke before dawn and lay in bed, watching the room brighten with a cold, grey light that filtered in from the city streets. Pushkin, through some infallible cat instinct, became aware of his wakefulness and leaped lightly to the bed, then walked with delicate feet up to his stomach. There he settled regally and started cleaning his paws.

Watching him, Clifford smiled, and then let his eyes wander up to the ceiling. He had relived the evening with Rhoda and Steve again and again during the night wondering how much was truth and how much deception.

That telepathy trick. He had seen similar stunts, all clever and all almost foolproof, but admittedly, none quite like this one. There had been no paraphernalia or codes. The truth was he hadn't wanted to accept it, or Steve's wild story, but he knew that in spite of his reluctance he believed in both.

Why? Why should anything that fantastic still have a ring of truth?

The answer lay with Anna he realized as the first cold sunlight touched his windows. He had believed Anna, and believing her he must accept the fact that Jack had actually changed into a wolf, that whatever Steve had done to his chromosomes had caused that change.

Believing this completely impossible situation, it had been easy to believe the rest. One foot into fairyland, he thought wryly, and the entire trip becomes a possibility. The telepathy, the league of pale-eyed women, and above all the plot to change Jack genetically.

Abruptly he jumped out of bed, ignoring Pushkin's aggrieved protests, and he headed for the shower. Somehow when Jack returned he had to head him off, warn him. When Jack returned! Didn't he mean if?

He spent the early morning in his studio, trying to lose himself in his work, but his mind kept wandering back to the girls, and then to Jack. What had happened to him? What did they intend to do to him?

Finally, at eleven o'clock, he threw down his pencil in disgust and shoved his hands into his pockets. The work would just have to wait. He had to do something, anything, but he couldn't stay cooped up here. Maybe he ought to see Steve again and find out exactly what she intended. No, not Steve. There was an ironlike core to her that would resist any pressure. She hadn't given an inch last night and she wouldn't now. But Rhoda. He was sure she would listen, that he could convince her.

Convince her of what? Just what did he want them to do, or not to do? What was he afraid of? Was it simply to leave Jack alone? To let him spend the last days of his life in peace, not as some impossible stud for a group of telepathic women? Or was it to tell him the truth, to let him know what they had done and what they intended to do?

Jack had thought his period as a wolf was an hallucination, mental decay before death. In that frame of mind wasn't he capable of something desperate, of suicide, of trying to meet death with dignity instead of through the dissolution of brain damage?

But it was more than that. Steve had hinted that Jack's change to what they wanted was only possible under stress. Were they capable of putting him in a situation where it was change or else—or else what? Death? Disaster? Rhoda wasn't, he thought, but Steve was surely capable of it.

He called Jack's number again, but there was still no answer. Not that he believed there would be. It was too long since he had last seen him. Something had obviously happened and he ought to report the whole matter to the police. They had routines for hunting missing men.

But if Jack was still alive, if for some reason he had deliberately chosen to disappear, would he want him to go to the police? But what possible reason could he have for disappearing?

He shook his head and sighed. Suppose the girls had lied and they had been in touch with Jack all along, putting him through whatever wild tests they had dreamed up. Suppose he was with them right now, and in danger?

Damn it, he had to know. Not only for Jack's sake, but for his own if he were to have another peaceful moment. He looked at his watch. Almost twelve. Steve would be at the medical school, but Rhoda was probably at home—wherever that was. They had given him no hint last night. How could he find out? He didn't think it was the city, but where else? The Island? Westchester? Connecticut?

He called the medical center and asked for personnel. He was trying to contact Dr. Douthright, he told them, did they have her address? Personnel put him through to her own department. Perhaps she was in and could help him.

He swore softly at his own lack of imagination. If Steve answered he'd hang up, but instead a pleasant-voiced secretary told him Dr. Douthright wasn't in the office just then. Relieved, Clifford said that was just fine. "You see, I want to send her a birthday card. I'm an old friend from Montreal and I know she's at Einstein, but I haven't her home address."

"I *am* sorry," the secretary said regretfully, "but we don't give out home addresses."

"Oh." Clifford cast about frantically. "I hate to write to her at the school . . ." He let a wistful note creep into his voice, and took a gamble. "Westchester covers a lot of territory."

There was a moment's silence, and then, uncertainly, the secretary said, "I think she's in South Salem, but I'm not sure and I really can't give the address out. I'm sorry."

He mustn't push it. "Well, thanks anyway. Bye." He hung up quickly and found that his hand was shaking. He wasn't much of a liar. In a moment he dialed South Salem information and got a new telephone number for Dr. Douthright, Barnyard Road, but no number.

All right. How long could Barnyard Road be? They had evidently taken a house in the country. If he could get up there now, before Steve came home from work, if he could have a little time alone with Rhoda he was sure he could get at the truth.

The first thing was a car. There was a car rental outfit near the river and they had a car in front of his house in half an hour. After he had signed the papers, he drove crosstown to the West Side Highway, and up into Westchester. He picked up a road map at a gas station and saw that this highway would lead him to the Hawthorne Circle; above that Route 23 went directly to South Salem on the Connecticut–New York border.

It was a long ride, a long commute for Steve too. Why had they picked a place this remote? Was there any significance to that?

It was late afternoon by the time he arrived at the narrow country road labelled Barnyard. Five mailboxes near the main road told him how many houses there were, and one had a freshly lettered Douthright-Watson on it.

He pulled into the driveway of the house at four o'clock. The cold, clean sky of the morning was overcast with grey, and a drab, white light covered the landscape. The house stood by itself on top of a small, treeless hill. Below it, in the valley, there was a twisting river that broadened out into a shallow swamp. The swamp, just below the house, ended at a dam, and a trickle over the spillway carried the river on down the valley.

The house itself was old, over two hundred years, he guessed, and the artist in him responded to the clean, white frame lines, the long windows and the crusting of gingerbread that decorated the porch. It had been remodeled, added to and redone a number of times, but always, whoever had worked on it had the good sense to leave the basic lines intact.

From the porch he looked back at a magnificent view of the road, the valley, the river and the distant, low hills.

There was no bell, but the simple front door had a massive brass knocker. He let it fall, and the sound reverberated through the house. It had hardly stopped before the door opened and he was facing Rhoda, a calm and unsurprised Rhoda.

Does anything shake her up or disturb her? he wondered, and felt a sudden overwhelming desire to ruffle her serenity in some way, to see that lovely composed face excited—and frightened.

He pushed the thought back and took his hat off. "Hello."

As if she were expecting him, she stood aside, holding the door open. "Come in and put your coat there." She nodded at

(157)

an elaborate coat rack in the front hall. "Steve isn't in, but of course—you know that."

Feeling guilty in spite of himself, he hung up his coat and followed her into a front parlor, an early American parlor of gleaming pine and ruffled organdy, handwoven upholstery and softly gleaming pewter plates. Wood panelling, painted white, reached shoulder height with a plate rail gracing it, and above the walls were painted a soft, whited green.

He nodded appreciatively. "It's a lovely house, and this room —perfect."

Rhoda smiled. "No thanks to us. We bought it decorated and furnished. Steve's been muttering about it ever since. I think she'd like to tear out the front wall, make a huge picture window and furnish it with Danish Modern. Can I get you something to drink?"

He shuddered at the Danish Modern. "No. At least not yet." He sat down in a bentwood rocker. "I wanted to talk to you."

She nodded. "I thought you would." She sat on a small loveseat opposite him and spread her skirt. He was aware that it was uncommonly long. The new midi look? But no, not quite. There was something of the thirties about her dress, yet it seemed as if she wore a completely new style, a style that dated back to a much earlier era. There was an illusion of hoops, of old-fashioned silks and velvets. Even her hair, drawn back in a bun, framing the lovely oval of her face, seemed to belong to some early American past.

There was a serenity about her that he could almost feel. The antagonism he had come with, the anger and indignation at Jack's supposed treatment, suddenly seemed ridiculous and out of place here.

Still she sat there waiting, and finally he said, "I've come about Jack."

"Yes, I realized that."

"What he's been through, what he may be going through now

—it's just not right or fair. I want you and Steve to understand that."

Rhoda spread her hands. "Perhaps that's so, Mr. McNally, but . . ."

"Clifford, please."

"Clifford then. Perhaps that's so, but Steve started something in Montreal that must be finished. I didn't agree with her at first, but now I'm sure she's right."

"You say it must be finished. How?"

She bit her lip a moment. "If Jack comes back—when Jack comes back—Steve has a series of tests. She wants to do chromosome studies, and then, if Jack is what she and the women who work with her believe, if he's genetically labile . . ." She paused to smile and shake her head. "Genetics is a field I know nothing about. Give me something to do with my hands, weaving, painting, sewing . . . but theoretical genetics! I'm lost."

He interrupted her rudely. "And if he's genetically labile, then what?"

Her smile flickered briefly, reluctantly, then disappeared. Her delicate eyebrows drew down over her pale eyes. "Steve has a test. I'll admit it's a dangerous one, maybe deadly. It's taking an awful chance, but she says if Jack can change, it must be when he's under some kind of stress. There must be some way to make him change to—to what we want, to make him allelomorphic for our own mutant gene. She's explained it to me with diagrams, but it doesn't register. I'm sorry, Clifford, I don't really know what she plans, and I think it has to be—well, it has to be kept from Jack too, in order to work."

She looked genuinely disturbed and he almost began an apologetic protest, when with a sudden chill he wondered if it weren't all an act, all designed to convince him that there was no way he could interfere with what they planned.

He stood up and walked to the window, pulling aside the organdy curtains to stare out at the valley and the river. There was something so genuinely honest about her. He didn't want to believe she was lying. If it were a lie, why had she told him this much?

"You can't play with a man like this," he protested. "You can't treat him as if he were a guinea pig or a mouse in a laboratory. Jack is a living, breathing man. You don't experiment with a man. Can't I make you two understand that?"

She stood up and came to him quickly. "Can't we make you understand what this means, not only to us, but to humanity? Jack is our only hope for tomorrow's man!"

The pretentiousness of it snapped him out of the spell she had cast around him. He looked at her in dismay, at her suddenly exalted look, the widened eyes and parted lips. Quite deliberately he said, "Balls to tomorrow's man—and woman too! My private opinion is that you're all a pack of dangerous nuts, and I'm going to do my damnedest to stop you."

Slowly the exalted look left her and her eyebrows drew down in a frown. "You won't be able to stop us, Clifford," she said flatly.

"We'll see about that." It seemed as melodramatic an exit line as her tomorrow's man bit, he thought. He jammed his hat on his head. "I never wanted to get involved in this, but I'm in it now for better or for worse." Was that what he really wanted to say? He was all muddled about the whole business. "I'm sticking with it. I owe that much to Jack." Whatever that was supposed to mean. A string of clichés were always easier to get out than real thoughts.

Even now, frowning but adamant, the tranquillity never left Rhoda. Thoughtfully she said, "That's what Steve meant, and she was right, about not having anything in common with men. There's a comprehension gap between us."

"You just bet there is," Clifford said savagely, "and maybe a gap between you and the rest of humanity."

She smiled sadly. "Perhaps there is a difference. There are

(160)

human concepts I can't understand, like murder or war."

He didn't answer, but slammed out of the house and almost ran down the hill to the car. Well, he had loused that up, and had gotten almost none of the information he had come for, nor had he convinced her of his point of view. "Whatever that is," he muttered.

As he pulled out of the driveway he could see her standing on the porch, slim and tall, her skirt whipped about her legs by the autumn wind, so lovely he could scarcely believe it.

He fumed and raged halfway back to the city, hardly understanding the depth of his anger or the cause of it. Was it Rhoda's constant reminder that she and Steve and the others like her were so obviously superior? Was that what galled him more than anything else?

It was true that he had no leg to stand on in talking about humanity. He laughed and shook his head. Man's inhumanity to man! What a stale old story, but it was more than that. What he resented was her calm assurance that they were right, that they had the privilege to submit Jack to tests, to poking and picking and prying.

In another few miles he was able to smile. Had Homo neanderthalensis felt the same way when Cro-Magnon men moved into his valleys and hunting fields? Now it was make way for Homo superiorensis—or something. Well, he was damned if he would. Somehow he'd manage to upset their little applecart. They'd have to damn well fight for this earth.

Come to think of it, there was nothing more terrible than the idea of a telepathic race of men. The last area of privacy would be gone, the last hiding place. The very thought of it sent cold chills through him. And how much of his fierce, unreasoning resistance to the whole plot was based on just that?

To hell with it. He was tired and hungry. Just let him get home, shower and go out for a good meal. Man's future could wait. His fate could hang in the balance.

(161)

But later, finishing his supper in a small French restaurant on Second Avenue, he kept remembering that afternoon, thinking of things he should have said, answers he should have given— and above all questions he should have asked.

He had called Jack again this evening, but there was still no answer, and now, settled over a cigar and coffee, he felt an uneasy apprehension about the whole thing.

He stubbed out the cigar angrily. It was unthinkable that this should bother him so, should intrude so on the ordered routine of his life. And it had been ordered, he thought, neat and carefully routinized. His world. The secure fortress of his apartment, and an occasional venture out into the East Side of Manhattan for dinner or a movie. Today, driving up to South Salem had been his first variation from an inflexible routine.

But he liked that routine. That was the point. He liked the day-to-day living, the certainty of it, his records and books and his cat. The only concession to sociability had been the rare evenings he and Jack had spent together. What was his relationship to Jack? What did he feel for him? Friendship? Something deeper than that? My only friend, he said in sudden wonder. It boils down to that. My only friend!

Why now did he have this terrible restlessness, this weary sense of apprehension? It was Rhoda, of course, and the whole damned mess this afternoon. What he needed, he realized with a start of surprise, what he desperately needed, was someone to talk to.

He paid his bill and left the restaurant, walking slowly through the darkened streets, dawdling in front of the brilliantly decorated windows of the antique shops. Was there anyone he could call, anyone he knew well enough to be at ease with, to talk out his problems?

No one really. One by one, and quite deliberately he had cut himself off from his friends, and he hadn't regretted it, nor did he really regret it now. The isolation was what he wanted and needed.

And then, surprisingly, he thought of Anna, of her disordered apartment and warm, comforting acceptance. Surely, by now she had gotten over her shock. By now she'd be willing to talk about Jack and the whole problem. He had only once seen Anna alone, without Jack. But she had been warm and friendly. Why not see her now?

But Anna, when he called, was busy. Regretfully. "It's so nice to hear from you, Clifford, and I would love to see you. Tonight it's just not possible. Another night?"

"Of course." He hung up despondently and continued his walk. He stepped into a movie house in the Seventies, but walked out halfway through the picture when the images on the screen made no sense, had no power to hold him or involve him in their shadow plot.

Involvement, he told himself on his way home, was what was so surprising about this business with Jack. How had he become so totally involved? In recent years he had taken pride in his ability to keep his life apart, infringing on no one, involving no one.

Abruptly, and with terrifying clarity, his mind flashed back to the days in New Orleans, to Sarah's terrifying suicide attempt, the frantic trip to the hospital, the endless wait and the final shocking report. "It wasn't the sleeping pills. We had her stomach pumped out in time, but the lungs, you see, somehow she had regurgitated into her lungs . . ."

He didn't see. Nor did he understand any of it except that Sarah's suicide attempt had succeeded indirectly. Relief and guilt, shame and horror were inextricably tied up within him. That was when he had sworn desperately that he would never be involved with any other life, that he would live apart, complete and sufficient to himself.

Damn it, it had worked. Perhaps his life was empty, but he could point to any number of involved people who led far emptier, far more desperate lives. Why then had he become so tied up in Jack's problems? Why couldn't he shut the whole thing out of his mind, out of his life and return to the calm of the days before Jack had called from the park?

He could and he would. Let him just reach Jack and warn him and he would wash his hands of the whole affair. "I'll wash that man right out of my hair!" He laughed for the first time that night and started for his apartment, walking swiftly and purposefully.

He called Jack before he went to bed, but there was still no answer, and the next morning, after a shower and shave he called once more, knowing the phone would ring unanswered.

But to his astonishment and delight it was answered by the third ring.

"Hello? Jack?"

"Clifford? Is that you?" Jack's voice was heavy and drugged with sleep.

"Thank God you're back! Are you all right? Where have you been, for Chrissakes? Why didn't you call or at least leave a message? I've been worried sick . . ."

"Clifford, Clifford . . ." A tremendous yawn. "I can't talk, Cliff. I got to sleep only a few hours ago, and I'm so groggy, so damned groggy. I couldn't call. It was like—like before. Cliff, can I call you back later, when I wake up? Please! You don't know how beat I am."

"Sure. It's okay. I just feel relieved as hell that you're back. I'll wait for your call."

He heard the line click in the middle of a tremendous yawn, and he smiled as he hung up. Well, thank heaven for that. What a load off his mind! Jack was safe. He'd speak to him later, and they'd get together this afternoon. He pushed the uneasy "like before" out of his mind. He'd tell Jack the whole crazy story and finally, oh, what a relief that would be, he'd be rid of it.

"I do not want to be my brother's keeper," he said firmly as he poured his coffee and slipped two slices of bread into the toaster.

Chapter Thirteen

Rᴴᴼᴰᴬ ʀᴇᴄᴇɪᴠᴇᴅ a call that same morning and replaced the phone slowly, standing motionless in front of the small table, staring with unseeing eyes out the wide living-room windows, down the sere hillside to the silvered snake of the river in the valley. Her face gave no indication of the turbulence inside her, the excitement that surged through her like a flood.

He was back. Then it must begin now, and quickly, before Clifford could start any trouble. The carpenters had finished in the back wing and there was no sign of their work. Nothing must go wrong now.

"Steve," she whispered softly. "Oh, Steve, you must be right. Dear God, I pray you're right!"

Then she picked up the phone and dialed Steve's office, and waited patiently for her to pick up the ringing phone.

Clifford worked as if possessed, doing more in one morning and part of the afternoon than he usually did in a week. His mind was totally immersed in the layouts, all his thoughts concentrated only on balance, shape, color and form, page after page.

It was only when the fading outside light made him reach for the switch to the fluorescent that he realized what time it was. More than half the afternoon had gone and he hadn't once thought of Jack, of Jack's problems or Rhoda and Steve, of grey-eyed telepathic women.

Smiling, he stacked the layouts, cleaning off the last traces of rubber cement with a pickup, then wrapped the package and called for a messenger. While he was waiting, he changed out of his work clothes, took a quick shower and had just finished dressing when the bell rang. He tipped the messenger, gave him the package and closed the door with a sigh of relief. His obligations were discharged. Instead of waiting for Jack's call he'd try him now. Surely he had slept long enough. He must be up and about.

He was awake and he answered on the second ring, but he was still in bed. "I don't think I'll ever get out of it," he said. "I'm going to bury myself in this bed and make up for—Cliff, how long have I been gone?"

"Three days. Jack, where have you been?"

There was a long silence, and then Jack sighed. "If I told you, you'd think I was crazy or lying. Cliff, come over, can you?"

"Try and keep me away. Get your story straight and put on some coffee. I'll be there in half an hour." He hung up and whistling cheerfully pulled on a turtleneck sweater and a jacket.

He'd be at Jack's before that if he could catch a cab quickly.

He started down the block and saw an empty taxi pull up at the corner. He flagged it and inside gave Jack's address, lifting his eyebrows at the back of the cabbie's head. Shoulder-length red hair tumbled over the neck of a blue sweater. He looked at the ID card through the bulletproof partition and saw a woman's name, Alice Marks.

"You don't see many women drivers these days. Isn't it a hard racket?"

She shrugged. "No harder than others." She had a pleasant, husky voice. "Keeps you out in the air."

She ran a red light across Fifth Avenue and cut into Central Park at 72nd Street. Suddenly aware of where they were, Clifford sat up and leaned forward. "Hey, I told you the East Side! Where are you going?"

She shook her head as she turned into the uptown drive in the park. "Sit down, buddy, and relax."

"What the hell is this?" He tapped on the glass partition. "Where do you think you're going?"

She turned and gave him a quick grin through the glass. "Where do *you* think we're going?"

That one quick glimpse was enough to see her eyes, pale grey, with almost no differentiation between iris and pupil, pale grey under heavy lashes, a lovely face, a frightening face.

He sat back and stared at the driver's mirror, meeting her calm, level gaze. "You're one of them, aren't you?"

He could only see her eyes, but he could tell she was smiling by her voice. "You make it sound like a federal offense."

"Isn't it? Kidnapping a man?"

"Taking you for a cab ride, baby. That's all. No one's going to hurt you. No one's going to abduct you."

She slowed down and came to a stop at a traffic light, and he wrenched at the door handle, trying to open it, but it held fast.

"Safety measure. Thank Mayor Lindsay. They lock from the

driver's seat." She turned round in the seat, an attractive, freckled, corn-fed face, a woman in her early thirties. She brushed her hair away from her eyes. "Why don't you relax?"

"Where are we going?"

"Over to the West Side for a little while. Maybe have a drink or two at a friend's place, and then you'll be free as a bird."

"A little while?" He shook his head. "Until you can get Jack out of his apartment? Damn it, let me out of here!"

She turned back and the car shot ahead as the light changed. "My word for today is relax."

Cursing furiously he worked the handles of both doors, but neither would budge nor could he lower the windows. Finally, in a rage, he started hammering at the glass partition between him and the driver.

"Don't worry about that," she called pleasantly over her shoulder. "These cabs are really holdup-proof—and a good thing, huh?"

"I'd like to wring your neck," he muttered. "Where are we going?" He sat back with folded arms, glowering sullenly at the back of her head.

"Now that's better," she said cheerfully. "When rape is inevitable, lean back and enjoy it. You know, I won't even charge you what's on the meter. Where do you get a ride like that these days?"

"Where are you taking me?"

"You're repeating yourself, pussycat. I told you, just across town. We want you to wait in a friend's apartment for just an hour or so. Now is that so hard—or awful? It's comfortable and there'll be good company."

He stared at the back of her head. "You're afraid I'll warn Jack."

"That's right. Now you stay put."

The cab left the park at 103rd Street and cut crosstown towards the drive. At one of the sidestreets it pulled up in front of a brownstone and the redhead turned to face him. She wasn't smiling now and she gestured towards the house. "We have a little reception committee and I wouldn't try anything silly if I were you. The girls are both ex-Wacs and very good shots, no matter how reluctant they are to prove it."

Two women were walking down the steps of the house, two ordinary women who could melt into any crowd with no trouble. Both were young and dressed in casual suits, one with a small pillbox of a hat and white gloves, the other with sleek black hair tumbling below her shoulders. They both carried sweaters, sweaters which quite casually covered their right hands. He had no doubt that the driver was right, that the sweaters covered two competent guns.

The redhead said, "The door is open now, the one at the curb side. Go into the house with them."

He tried to salvage a shred of dignity as he climbed out. "Well, thanks for the ride."

"It was a pleasure. I'll look for you while I'm cruising."

"Yeah, you do that." He straightened out, standing on the sidewalk, and now, very naturally it seemed, both of the women were flanking him, both smiling eagerly, a pleasant little street tableau.

"We're so glad you could come," the one with the hat said, the one on his right. The black-haired one on his left shoved her gun forward until it touched his body. He winced away from it, and automatically started towards the steps. The one with the hat took his arm, for all the world like an old friend, and began to chatter brightly as they moved up the steps. "It was such a trip too, all the way from across town, and it isn't as if it were the nicest day, did you see how the sun just clouded over? Margaret, it was a day just like this in Cleveland when Jenny came down with the flu . . ."

He never liked anyone touching him. Physical contact always made him tense and uneasy, and the touch of this woman's arm

(169)

set his teeth on edge. But the gun on his left overcame his objections effectively, and he climbed the steps quietly between the two. At the top he glanced down over his shoulder and saw the redhead leaning casually against the cab, tall and slim in tight jeans and a blue sweater. She raised one hand in a mocking salute, then bent to her taxi.

The woman on his left, Margaret? was bent over opening the door with a key, and he had a wild impulse to shove her aside, tear loose from the other's arm and run.

Softly, as if reading his thoughts, no longer the eager gossiper, the woman with the hat said, "I wouldn't. We'd nail you before you could reach the street." The door was open now and Margaret was waiting silently, a half smile on her face. He looked at her eyes, grey from iris to pupil, then at the other with the same eyes in a totally different face, and with a little shiver he nodded and moved forward.

But whatever they think they're getting away with, they're wrong, he told himself fiercely. I'll get out of this somehow, damn them both!

The hall was dimly lit, and a narrow wooden staircase and bannister ran up the right side. The woman holding his arm let go and pushed him forward gently. "Upstairs."

"Now just a minute." He turned towards them. "What the hell is going on? What right have you to push me around like this?"

There were no smiles now, but both of them, almost casually, removed the sweaters and he stood there looking into two small but deadly guns. It was a horrifying moment. The sight of the two guns melted his aggression and he moved back, stumbling against the stairs. He was no hero! How he knew that in this moment.

The one called Margaret said, "You will go upstairs with us and we'll wait for an hour. That's all. Then you'll be free to go, Mr. McNally, and please, no heroics."

"Why do you want me here for an hour? Because of what I might tell Jack?"

She shrugged. "We won't answer your questions. Please. Upstairs."

He stood there for a moment longer, staring at the two guns, then he turned and started to climb the stairs, the two of them right behind him, single file.

No, he was no hero. He hadn't the nerve to question the guns, to throw himself at the girls as they did in the movies and assert his virility and manhood with a few well-placed karate chops. He felt a fine beading of sweat on his forehead and he knew that whatever they wanted he would do, quite obediently.

And that might have been the end of it, except that the building was old and the staircase very narrow, the carpeting threadbare and worn. Halfway up, with both the women lined up behind him, he caught his heel on the carpet and stumbled. He churned the air wildly with one hand, the other clutching for the bannister and heard one of the women cry out, "Careful, watch out!"

The other one yelled, "Damn it, don't be so clumsy!"

He could have recovered his balance, but that "clumsy" did it, igniting a flicker of defiance. The hell with it. Let the accident take its course!

He deliberately missed the bannister, gave a wild shout and flung himself backwards down the staircase. He smashed into the woman directly behind him. She let out her breath in a startled gasp, struggled for balance, and then the two of them crashed down on the second woman. There was one horrifyingly loud shot as her gun went off, and then the three were tumbling down the staircase, one on top of the other.

Clifford, by some miracle of balance, landed upright on top of the heap, and without even thinking, let the impetus of his fall carry him forward, half staggering, half running down the hall. He tore open the door and took the steps of the stoop two at a

(171)

time, then pelted furiously towards the corner.

Almost at the corner he heard shouting behind him, and he looked back to see the two of them racing down the steps, but their guns were out of sight. Then he was around the corner on a broad avenue. It was a short block to the next downtown cross street, and he loped towards it, the people in the street stopping to stare at him. If he could reach it before they saw him, he would duck down it and head west towards Riverside Drive. He could catch a cab there.

He thought of that other cab ride, but surely they couldn't arrange something like that again! How many women could they have driving cabs?

A woman turned the corner ahead of him, coming towards him quickly, not looking at him, and that alone was peculiar. Everyone else on the street was staring. He slowed to a walk and stopped as she came on. If he could only see her eyes. Then he looked back and cursed softly. The first two had turned the corner.

He stood there for a moment, confused, and then realized that in a moment the three converging women would reach him. He could see the woman ahead clearly now and with a cold chill noticed her eyes, pale grey.

She was beginning to run towards him, and suddenly he turned and took off across the avenue, cutting directly in front of a car and missing it by inches. He heard brakes squeal, a horn blow, and then he was across. But the block was still a trap. They were all three crossing now. He couldn't possibly reach a side street in time.

There was an apartment building in the center of the block and he ran towards it, pulling open the outer door, and then, to his horror, found that the inner door was locked. Frantically he turned to the row of bells and began to punch them, all of them, hoping at least one would answer before the women reached the building.

(172)

Looking out of the glass-panelled front door he could see them approaching the building. He rattled the inner door frantically, and then, just as they started up the steps, the buzzer sounded.

He pulled the door open and ducked inside, into a wide lobby with an elevator at one end and a stairway at the other. The elevator was closed and he didn't dare wait. He ran to the stairway. Upstairs would trap him, but behind the steps a flight led down to the basement, and halfway down a door opened into a rear yard.

He raced down the half flight, tore open the door and stumbled out into an alley filled with ashcans. The alley ran behind two houses that were back to back, and like the sides of an H, two side alleys led from the avenue he had just come from to the next street over. If he could duck back to that avenue while they were still inside—

But when he reached the side alley, a dim tunnelled stretch, he realized that they had anticipated him. He heard the quick tap of high heels coming from the avenue. Without hesitation he turned in the other direction and raced forward, towards the next street over.

Halfway down the alley there was a door into the second house. He tugged at it, and as it opened twisted inside. There had to be another entrance and they couldn't possibly head him off here. But then he couldn't understand the trick at the alley. How had they signalled to one another?

As he groped through the darkness of a trunk room, it suddenly hit him. The telepathy Steve had explained to him, the parlor trick, only it wasn't a trick. They were all like that, of course, all able to communicate instantly with each other, around corners, out of sight . . . it didn't matter. In effect, however many there were, they might just as well be monitoring the place with highly efficient walkie-talkies.

But how many could there be? They couldn't have been this

(173)

prepared, couldn't have known he'd escape the first time. Had the third woman, coming around the corner at just that moment, been coincidence, or had she been put there as a safeguard, or even signalled out of hiding?

He pulled open another door to find himself in a vast deserted boiler room. Huge tanks threw off waves of heat and a tumbled mass of pipes twisted overhead in the half gloom of the ceiling.

Somewhere there had to be a door, but probably not on ground level. He moved forward slowly, and then froze as he heard a door open across the room and footsteps tap against metal. Someone had come into the boiler room from the building and was climbing down a flight of metal steps. But how could they have possibly followed him this quickly? Were they omnipotent?

The steps came towards him, not stealthy but assured and familiar. He moved around the boiler, wincing as he touched the hot metal. If they knew he was here, they had him trapped.

He was halfway around the boiler when he heard the storeroom door he had come in by open. This was it. There were two of them now. He tensed himself, and then to his amazement heard a man's voice, puzzled and annoyed. "Now what you doing down here, miss?"

A woman, it sounded like Margaret, answered brightly and not at all startled. You would swear she had just wandered in by chance. "I was looking for a way up from the storage room. Isn't there another exit?"

He was all the way around the boiler now, facing the exit the man had come in by, a flight of metal steps with a door ajar at the top. It must be the superintendent who had come this way and caught Margaret.

He heard the man's voice again, slightly exasperated, but not quite so annoyed. The charm was working. "Now tenants ain't

(174)

allowed down here. It's against the safety rules. You can't cross this way."

He raced silently up the metal stairs, ducked through the half-open door, hearing the woman protesting gently behind him. So natural, so normal. It scared the hell out of him. Damn them, they were so cool and casual, always ready with an easy explanation and probably even while she explained signalling to another one to get around to the front of the building.

He was in another hallway with a door opening from it, still in the basement, and halfway down he saw a glass-panelled door with a red exit light. He ran towards it, hurried through, then up another half flight and out into the building's lobby.

The lobby was filled with women and children, school children, obviously. The laughter, the chattering, all hit him like a solid wall, and he hesitated, ready to turn back. Were any of these women—they?

But these were normal women, surely, housewives, mothers. School must have just let out. He forced himself forward, pushing through the crowd. They were waiting for the elevators, he realized. Then he was through the wide front doors and out in the street, Broadway by the look of it. He felt his whole body covered with sweat and he drew in a deep breath of air. The West Side. Christ, he didn't know it at all. He couldn't remember the last time he had come over here.

But he stood there for only a moment, trying to calm his racing heart, and then, a block away, he saw the kiosk of a subway station. If he could only get there, they couldn't possibly follow him through a crowded subway.

He began to jog along, dodging around people in the crowded street. He didn't dare look behind. He realized how conspicuous the jogging must be, and he slowed down to a walk. How much about him could they signal to each other? Not all of them knew what he looked like. Could they send mental pictures, or descriptions? What was the range of their telepathy anyway?

Someone caught at his arm, and he dodged aside in sudden panic. But it was a man, a panhandler. "Please. Yuh got the price of a cuppa coffee?"

"No, no—I'm in a hurry." He ducked past and hurried his pace. As always, when he refused a panhandler, he had a quick stab of guilt. What would it have cost to give him a few coins? And it might have brought him luck—Christ, he needed luck now! He actually hesitated, half turning back, and then shook his head. Was he out of his mind? The light at the corner was just changing to red and he raced across, beating the oncoming cars by inches. The subway steps were ahead of him and a group of school children were surging up leaving no room to get by.

He shoved and pushed his way down till he reached the change booth, and then he fumbled in his pocket for change. He seemed to have nothing but pennies, and finally he shoved a dollar bill at the woman in the booth.

"How many?"

What were they, 20 cents each? It had been so long since he had ridden the subway. "Let me have five?"

"Only two to a customer."

"Okay, two." He took the tokens and change. Was she deliberately trying to delay him? He looked at her face, waiting for her to raise her eyes from the newspaper she was reading inside the booth. When she looked up, she frowned out of annoyed, black eyes. "Well?"

"Nothing." He turned to the turnstiles and pushed through, then hurried to the downtown platform. It was almost empty while a train on the other side was discharging a wild, shouting mob of children. Christ, how many school children were there?

He paced down the platform nervously. Where was the damned train? There was only one old man on the platform, busily poking through the trash container, sorting out the scattered pages of the discarded afternoon papers.

If the train would only come now he'd be rid of them. Damn it, where was it? He paced down the platform to the far end where a post offered some concealment. Maybe they'd miss him if they looked down the platform. Maybe he could get on the train without their knowing it.

A slow rumbling filled the subway and down the platform the lights of an oncoming train swelled and filled the tunnel. "Hurry, hurry!" he whispered.

Then, as it thundered to a stop and the doors opened, he looked back. Two women were running to catch it, one waving an umbrella, the other carrying a shopping bag.

They couldn't be connected with the grey-eyed ones. They didn't even look up the platform but dashed for the doors. He stepped into the train just before the doors closed, pushing past the crowd that blocked the doorway. The two women had already boarded the train at the far end of the platform. No, they were no part of the chase.

He let out his breath in a sigh of relief. He had outwitted them all right, there was no way they could get to him now. He'd get out at the next station and take a cab crosstown. Or would he? A cab. He shook his head, remembering the red-headed Alice Marks. No. He'd stay on down to Times Square and shuttle across to the East Side. It was quicker and safer.

But at Times Square he decided that the wisest thing was to call Jack first. Then if anything happened to him he'd at least have warned him. He fumbled in his pockets for coins and dialed the number. It rang twice, and then a beep and a voice, obviously recorded, cut in. "The number you have dialed is not a working number. I am sorry. Please check your directory or call the operator for assistance. Thank you . . ."

He hung up and bit his lip. Had he dialed wrong in his hurry? He tried it again carefully, and again heard, "The number you have dialed . . ."

He hung up slowly, feeling the cold fear touch his back. They had managed this somehow, anticipating his move, every move. What were they? How had they done it?

He looked around at the hurrying press of people. Any one of the women rushing past him could belong to them, old, young, Negro, white . . . Was there any guarantee he had eluded them? Couldn't they always alert one of their own kind, broadcast his description, whip up a net to trap and hold him anywhere in the city?

This was ridiculous. He had eluded them. This was nothing but a foolish panic. He joined the crowd moving to the shuttle and pushed in. There was no possible way of tracing him in this mob.

He moved into the car and caught one of the hanging straps as the shuttle lurched away from Times Square towards Grand Central. He almost fell on top of an elderly woman reading the afternoon paper. She pulled it back with a show of annoyance and he mumbled an inarticulate apology.

As the train reached Grand Central he turned to join the shoving crowd leaving the shuttle. But he looked back just before he left the car and he saw her lower the paper and look up at him, a little old lady, white-haired and delicate, with the palest grey eyes, knowing eyes, washed of all color and emotion. She just sat there staring at him as the crowd pushed around him and then moved him with it off the train.

That was the worst part of it. She hadn't gotten to her feet. She hadn't rushed after him. She had just watched with that unbelievable calm. There was no need to move, she seemed to say. She could signal ahead of him, warn whoever was on the platform that he was coming, describe every detail about him.

Oh, God! He pulled free of the crowd and raced down the platform, colliding with the oncoming people carelessly. There was an arcade, and then an exit, and he tore through it and up a flight of marble steps, to find himself in the center of Grand

Central terminal. Again he jostled through the crowd, running for the street before he realized what he was doing and slowed down. But so many others were running here, to catch trains, to make cabs. Would he stand out that much? And what difference did it make, he thought defeatedly. They had followed him this far—how could he shake them?

But he had been so sure, so confident. How had they done it? The two women at the last moment in the subway? Was there nowhere they couldn't track him down? Or was there a safe place? Was that part of their plan, to convince him that he couldn't escape. Was that why the little old lady had sat so quietly?

He took off his hat and wiped his head with his handkerchief. It was covered with sweat and his hands were trembling. God, I'm a mess. He forced himself to stop. Take it easy. Relax. Think. Can they follow me everywhere? Use your brains. Think. Think!

There must be a weakness, there had to be, and standing there, drawing in deep breaths, he suddenly realized what it was. They were women, all women, and he was a man.

Across the room he saw a men's room sign, and he suddenly remembered one drunken evening with a crowd of friends catching a train for Westchester. Where was it, Mamaroneck? It was about ten years ago. One of them had gone to the men's room with him and they had come out a different exit, so completely different they were both confused and wandered about for fifteen minutes before they found the crowd.

Now which men's room was it? Which entrance? He bit his lip. This one? No. There was one on a mid-level, between the upper and lower terminal, and it exited on the upper level as well. He glanced around the huge room and slowly memory came back. There, by the right, near the exit. He put his hat back on and walked to the exit carefully. No panic now.

The men's room entrance was past a liquor shop and opposite

(179)

a bank of telephones. Half the phone booths were filled. Was one of the women in them grey-eyed? He walked through the exit and down a half flight of steps. This was one place they couldn't follow him, one place he could be secure in.

He had an overwhelming urge to urinate and he stepped up to one of the urinals to relieve himself. There was a man on either side, and he looked at their faces quickly. What guarantee did he have that they were really men? He finished and walked away. It was almost funny when you thought of it. No, he was safe here. He was sure of that.

He washed calmly and then hurried up the long flight of steps to the other exit. It led to a small waiting room and then out to the street. Did they know that? Unless you were a man, how could you possibly know the men's room had two exits? No. They must still be waiting at the other exit.

Outside there was a line of cabs and he caught the first one, a male driver he noticed thankfully, gave Jack's address and then sank back in exhaustion. He had done it. He had shaken them. They weren't, after all, infallible.

He had a vision of them waiting patiently outside the men's room, one joining the other, young women, old women, the whole army who had trailed him, waiting and studying each man as he left. He smiled at the picture, almost laughed out loud in sudden exhilaration.

At Jack's he paid the cab and hurried inside, taking the steps two at a time. He rang the bell and waited, then rang it again, and finally, in growing panic, put his finger on it and kept it there.

Andy, the super, came out with a mop and pail and recognized him. "You looking for Mr. Freeman?"

"Did you see him, Andy?"

Andy nodded at the street. "Just went out, about ten minutes ago."

"Alone?"

"Nooo—with a real cute dish." Andy grinned wickedly. "You single guys!"

As Clifford turned away and went down the steps slowly, he asked, "Should I tell him you called?"

"No. Don't bother, Andy." He stared hopelessly up and down the street as he remembered what the redheaded driver had said. "Just for an hour."

What a prize damned fool he had been. They had wanted an hour and he had given it to them, playing hide-and-seek all over the city while they had just the time they needed to get Jack away. It was funny when you thought about it, and as frightening as hell.

Chapter Fourteen

SLEEP, FOR JACK, was at first an endless, roaring vortex into which he slipped helplessly, a dark and deafening whirlpool that rose to a crescendo of tortured sound and then abruptly faded away to leave him floating on the oily waters of a sea bounded by a brazen bowl of sky. He floated belly up and struggled helplessly to open his eyes, but even with eyes closed he could see himself, disembowelled, swollen and baking under the heat that poured down from above.

He struggled to move, to pull his trailing entrails back with his paralyzed hands, to stem the slow ebb of blood that stained the water. And then, cutting lazy ripples in the surface scum, he saw the fins converging towards him, the shark pack summoned to the feast. He screamed but no sound came from his parched lips. Again and again he forced the soundless screams from his throat, and then he was fighting his way out of sleep, moaning and whimpering as he came awake.

He lay in a bath of sweat, too weak, too sick to get out of bed, and slowly he sank back into a dreamless, sodden sleep. He slept heavily and motionless long into the day. He woke just before Clifford's call, and he lay in bed, breathing harshly, staring around the room with frightened eyes, fighting to calm his racing heart.

The room was familiar, and yet so strange. But the strangeness lay in himself, not in the room. How empty it was, how devoid of all feeling! He felt a revulsion at the white walls, bone white, bleached of all meaning, as empty as a skeleton. No pictures, no drapes—a ghost of a room. And yet for so long he had lived here and accepted the emptiness.

He began to breathe more easily, and he wiped the sweat from his forehead. He wondered for a moment if it had all been a dream, a nightmare from which he was only now waking. He reached down to touch his chest, his body, and he shuddered. No. It was real, horribly real.

He shut his eyes and clenched his jaws, fighting down an overwhelming desire to scream.

The phone rang and Clifford's voice was the reassurance he needed to clutch at sanity. Afterwards he got out of bed and put on a bathrobe. He plugged in the electric coffeepot and then lit a small cigar, coughing as he drew in a mouthful of smoke, frowning at the unfamiliar, harsh taste.

He stared, uncomprehendingly, at the cigar in his fingers, then stubbed it out thoughtfully and started for the bathroom to shave and shower. The buzzer interrupted him and he answered it, expecting Clifford. To his amazement Rhoda walked in.

"Rhoda!" He stared at her, bewildered and yet delighted. "How did you find me?"

She smiled. "Jack! It's so good to see you. How do you feel?"

"Is it really you? Let me look at you. My God, it's been so long, or it seems that way. How did you find out where I live?"

"From the phone book." She stood just inside the door. "Are you glad to see me?" That faint smile, tender, enigmatic, almost mocking.

"You know I am!" Unexpectedly his throat was full and tight. He took her coat and suddenly conscious of his bathrobe pulled the belt tight. "I've thought of you two so often. Is Steve all right? Did she get that mess with Stiener straightened out?"

"Oh, that." She dismissed it with a wave of her hand. "She quit and came to New York. She has a wonderful spot at the Albert Einstein Medical Center. Jack . . . you've changed. Let me look at you. Your face . . ."

He stood facing her and tried to keep his voice light. "Changed for the better or worse?"

Softly she asked, "Has it been bad?"

It took him a moment to realize she meant the cancer. "That hasn't bothered me," he said in surprise. "Maybe Steve's DNA worked. Rhoda, so much has happened, so much I can't begin to explain. I have to talk this all over with someone, or I'll go out of my mind—if I haven't already. Where is Steve?"

"She's downstairs, circling the block in our car. It's a glorious day out, Jack. How would you like to take a ride up to Westchester?"

"Westchester?"

"South Salem. Steve and I have a house there. It's wonderful fall weather, just right for a day in the country, and we've all so much to talk about . . ."

He nodded slowly, staring at her. "I'd like that." A day in the country after the past frightening week! It sounded like heaven. He began to smile. She looked so lovely, more beautiful than he

(184)

had remembered. Those fantastic eyes and that hair. "Rhoda!" Impulsively he reached out and took her hands. "I've missed you."

"And we've missed you." She freed one hand and touched his chest through the half-open robe. The touch of her fingers against his bare skin went through his body like a shock. Harshly, he asked, "We?"

"I've missed you . . . so much." She bit her lip. "Jack, please put some clothes on."

He smiled and pulled her to him. She came easily, her lips lifting to his, her mouth sweet and fresh and unbearably soft. They clung together for almost a minute, then she pulled away reluctantly, her eyes glowing. "Steve's waiting, Jack."

"I have to shower." He remembered Clifford all at once. "Oh, damn, a friend of mine is coming up in a few minutes."

"We'll bring him along. It is a he?" When he nodded, she grinned. "An extra man is always welcome. You take your shower."

He showered leisurely, letting the scalding water wash over him, soaping and rinsing, again and again. So much brine and sea slime had dried on his skin. He didn't think he'd ever get it clean.

Finally, knowing Rhoda was waiting, he stepped out and towelled himself dry. Afterwards he inspected himself in the bathroom mirror. What he had seen in the train's lavatory was still unchanged. This body simply wasn't his—and yet it was. A birthmark on the side of his chest was unchanged, but his appendectomy scar was gone. He had a foreskin, but the shape, the size of his penis was the same. The color of his hair, the placement of body hair, it was all as it had been, and yet . . .

It was he as he might have been had he made a fetish of body care. It was a beautiful body, developed to the peak of physical perfection, and still it was his own. He dressed in the bathroom and came out to the fragrant odor of coffee and toast. From the kitchen Rhoda called out, "Your bread is stale, but I managed some toast from the center of the loaf. Poor Steve, I hope she hasn't given us up for lost. This is the most barren kitchen I've ever seen! Not even milk or butter."

"I take my coffee black. Anyway, I don't eat at home often." He struggled with the knot of his tie as he sipped the coffee. "My clothes are all falling off me. Any sign of Clifford?"

"I'm sorry, I forgot." Rhoda struck her forehead. "Your friend Clifford, he called while you were in the shower. Something about a sudden assignment. He said you'll understand and he'll see you tomorrow. Here, let me fix your tie."

She reknotted it, and having her that close he couldn't help but pull her into his arms again. "We'd better get started," she murmured reluctantly. "Steve will be ready to boil over. She has a low boiling point anyway."

Downstairs, he nodded to Andy and hesitated at the mailbox. "I haven't checked my mail in almost a week."

"Save it for tomorrow." She tugged at his arm and he followed her down the front steps. Steve had the car at the corner and they ducked inside, Jack in front and Rhoda in the back. It was an old MG, dark green and square nosed, and Steve handled it efficiently and with dash. She cut through city traffic recklessly and swung into the drive at 72nd Street, then caught the West Side Highway near the bridge.

Except for a brief hello, Jack had been silent till then, but now he turned to look back at the looming tower of the George Washington Bridge and said, "I jumped off that three days ago. I tried to commit suicide."

Rhoda caught her breath in a quick gasp, and Steve looked sideways at him, her grey eyes narrowed, a cigarette dangling from the corner of her mouth. "You're putting us on."

Jack sighed. "I wish I were. Steve, I want you to level with me about that stuff you gave me. It wasn't just DNA, was it?"

"DNA and a little bit more. Why?"

As Jack hesitated she said, "You tell me your dream and I'll tell you mine. Remember that old song? We've got a nice long drive ahead of us, Jack. Tell me what's happened to you and then I'll tell you everything about the DNA."

"Okay." He settled back. "Just do me one favor. Stop driving as if you were out for the Grand Prix and stay inside the speed limit."

Surprisingly, Steve slowed down to 45. "All right. Let's have it."

"The whole thing is fantastic and I don't know how to begin explaining it, or for that matter even believing it myself, unless you gave me something a hell of a lot stronger than DNA. Look." He unbuttoned his jacket and then his shirt, pulling them both away from his bare chest. "You saw my chest in Montreal, Steve, when you gave me the injection. You even kidded me about it. Did I have a chest like this then? How old am I, Steve? How old do I look?"

She glanced at him and then back at the road. "Tell me what happened," she said gently.

He began with his night of drinking and his visit to Anna, and afterwards his night in the park. "I changed, I really changed. It wasn't an illusion, or if it was, then hell, this is an illusion too. Everything is an illusion."

Slowly, fumbling for the right words, he talked on, telling them of his decision to commit suicide. "Maybe I was just sick and tired and frightened, getting nowhere. I don't know. It seemed, all of a sudden, a much cleaner and more decent way to go. It would at least be my own decision, my own choice made while I was still in control of my mind.

"Did I jump? I don't really know. I honestly don't. I think I did and I think that halfway down I changed my mind and suddenly, with all my heart, I wanted to live. My body obliged and I became a bird, all hundred and seventy pounds of me, a big-assed, clumsy bird that could hardly fly."

(187)

He told them of the struggle in the water, of his change to a shark, his days in the ocean, joining the pack and attacking the whale. "That was probably the most frightening part of it. As a man I like whales. They seem amusing and friendly animals. As a shark there was no concept of like or friendliness, no emotion such as amusement. I would have torn one of the pack apart if he had been wounded, cannibalized my own kind."

. He told them of his final capture, hooked for a tuna, and then what had happened last night. "I turned back to a man, but the man I might have been if I had grown up with every part of my body perfectly developed, just as I was a perfect shark and a perfect wolf. Steve," he looked at her with burning eyes, "am I crazy? Up in Montreal you hinted about a rat that had changed. I don't know what you meant, but could it have changed into— well, something small enough, or thin enough to escape its cage?"

She nodded heavily. "Yes, it could and it did. It changed into a snake. It was a wild rat I had given DNA and some chemical treatment. Jack, I believe your story, every part of it. I expected the changes, but I didn't think it would happen this way, or so quickly. I thought we'd have time to come down from Canada leisurely, get settled and look you up before anything took effect. It was a month before it worked on the rat, or . . . maybe it was a month before it had any reason to change."

"But how? That's what I've asked myself a hundred times. How can I change? How is it possible?"

"You are," Steve said carefully, "in a genetically labile state. I don't know if it's permanent or temporary, I just don't know. What I did, and I might as well be honest about it, was to give you an artificial DNA along with a number of other substances designed to weaken the genetic bonds in your chromosomes. It's an approach that's just being considered theoretically, a form of genetic engineering. We went one better than theory, and we've used it experimentally a hundred times on animals."

(188)

"We? You and Stiener?"

"Stiener knew nothing of the work. I had three women lab assistants who were all . . . interested, personally involved even as I was. We were all working without Stiener's knowledge. We were after something."

"After what? Steve, there's a hell of a lot more behind this than I'm aware of. What is it? What's going on?"

Steve had pulled off Route 23, and now she turned into Barnyard Road. "Let's have a drink first and then I'll give you a story right back, one to match yours and maybe outdo it."

They climbed out of the car and Steve stretched and grimaced. "God, I'm old and stiff. That car gets more like a torture box each trip."

"I told you to buy a civilized car and a late model," Rhoda said in annoyance. "We can afford it, but no, not you. It had to be an antique MG! Come on, Jack. Let's get inside."

But he paused on the porch and looked around, suddenly aware of where they were, of the country around him and the graceful white house. "This is nice. How long have you been here?"

"Since Steve started at the Medical Center. Wait till spring and she starts gardening. Back in Montreal we only had a tiny backyard, but here she can really go wild."

He remembered Steve's garden and smiled, then followed Rhoda into the house. The odor of roasting turkey filled it, and he drew in his breath hungrily. "Mmm! That smells good."

An elderly woman with grey hair and a flowered apron came in from the kitchen. "Back already? Did everything go all right?"

"Just fine, Allie. This is Jack. Jack, our—housekeeper." She hesitated just a moment over the title, and Allie smiled pleasantly and wiped her hands on the apron. Jack took her hand, frowning at her grey, pleasant eyes.

After she left, with a vague excuse about the meal, he turned

(189)

to Rhoda and Steve. "What is this with grey eyes, all three of you?"

"And thereby hangs our tale." Steve went to the sideboard and took out a bottle. "Scotch all around?"

"Fine. Look, you tell me your dream. I've already told you mine."

"Fair enough." Steve handed them drinks, then walked across the room to the windows. "And let me warn you, my dream's a lulu." She took a long swallow and blew out her breath. "That's good stuff." She faced Jack, her back to the window.

"If you could change so easily . . ."

"Easily!"

"Well, change at all. But let me make a confession first and then tell you a story."

"A confession?"

"Which you've probably guessed. The drugs I gave you with the DNA, I gave you only partly because of the cancer."

He heard the word *cancer* with something of a shock. It had been so long since he had felt any evidence of it, any pain at all, so long since he had brooded about it that now he found that he couldn't really accept the fact that he still might have it. "I don't know about the cancer," he said with a frown. "I plan to see a doctor about it as soon as possible."

Looking at him over the edge of the glass, Steve asked, "Have there been any new symptoms? Any bleeding? Has the pain gotten worse?"

"That's just it. The pain has disappeared, but it's more than the pain. It's my whole . . ." He reached up his hand in a grasping motion as if trying to take hold of the word. "It's my whole state of being. I feel so different."

Steve nodded. "You probably are different, not sick any more. Jack, after this period of time the pain should be overwhelming. If it's gone, it means that the cancer's gone too. We'll get you to a doctor tomorrow. I know a good man at Sloan-Kettering, but

(190)

he'll only confirm what I've said."

And in his heart he knew she was right. Whatever the change, he was sure it had cured him.

She chewed her lower lip a moment, then said, "But let me be honest. I only half expected the experiment to work."

"You warned me of that."

"Yes, but I didn't warn you that you might change, and I knew it, or should have guessed it."

He frowned at her. "That's what you mean by genetically labile."

She drew a deep breath. "I told this story to your friend Clifford a couple of nights ago."

"You've seen Clifford?"

"Yes. He looked us up when you were missing, thinking we might have seen you. Let me tell you the story I told him, the story of Rhoda and myself."

She began to talk then, telling again the story of the death of her father, the strange revelation of her telepathic ability, the Mexican girl and then finally how she found Rhoda—and the others.

Staring at her when she finished, Jack nodded towards the kitchen and Allie. "She's one of you too? One of your grey-eyed women?"

Steve nodded. "There are quite a few of us here in the New York area. Somehow or other we drift together, and a lot of us work in the biological sciences. Maybe it's a talent we inherit with our eyes, or maybe we're just damned interested in anything that might help. There are almost two dozen of us in microbiology and twice that number in genetics all over the country, but most of us hold other jobs. But enough of us have been involved in science to really work on this DNA problem."

"But why?"

"Is that so hard to understand? We are a handful of women, and there is no chance of a man turning up naturally with this mutant gene. We felt that the only answer lay in genetic manipulation."

Allie came into the living room and switched on a table lamp. "Dinner's ready now. Come in."

Rhoda went back to the kitchen with Allie to help with the serving, and Jack followed Steve to the table, slightly dazed and bewildered. "I still don't understand what you were after."

"Do you know anything about genetics?"

"A little. I know that the chromosomes carry the pattern of what we are, the blueprint, and that DNA is simply a tremendously long molecular chain. I know that sections of the chain are genes. I guess any schoolboy knows that. I've seen models of the construction of the DNA strand, and that's about it, except for the basic facts of inheritance."

Allie and Rhoda brought the food to the table, the turkey already sliced on a platter, and they both sat down and started passing the food around. Remembering the telepathy Steve had talked about, Jack watched the almost flawless way that one woman would reach for a plate before the other woman had quite passed it. He could easily believe in an undercurrent of communication, a level he had no part of

"What you know about the gene is correct," Steve picked up the conversation as she ate. "The DNA molecule is just a long chain made of different combinations of rings of phosphoric acid, a sugar called deoxyribose and purines and two pyrimidines. The purines and pyrimidines can be arranged in practically an infinity of different combinations."

"Have some squash," Rhoda said. "Allie baked it with brown sugar and pineapple."

He helped himself, and Steve said, "Ordinarily the DNA chain is pretty tight and needs something like radiation to break it and rearrange it, to produce what we call a mutation, a mutant gene. Actually, there are two types of genes, the primary genes which determine the structure of enzymes and other proteins and the regulatory genes, which control the activities of the primary genes. When we need the products that these genes manufacture, enzymes for example, the body is able to regulate their action, turn them off or on. No one knows how the body regulates this, but we've worked on the principle that certain chemical agents, some hormones, are the regulating agents. They can repress the activity of an undesirable gene and reactivate a desired gene."

She paused to help herself to more turkey, and Allie handed Jack a plate of tiny buttered carrots. "Try these, they're glazed with gelatin." He helped himself liberally, realizing that for the first time since he had been "hooked" he had no nausea at the taste of food.

"We've developed a fine mixture of hormones and chemicals," Steve went on, "that can repress and reactivate at will. We've redesigned and synthesized primary and regulatory genes too, and we've even incorporated them into chromosomes. That's genetic engineering. But the controlling factor, the factor men use unconsiously to 'work' their genes, that's escaped us. We haven't isolated it yet. We can make an organism genetiacally labile, but we could never control the change. You have that control."

"Me?" He put his fork down and stared at her. "You mean that's why I can change? When I came out of the ocean, I could only think of lycanthropy."

"What's that?" Allie asked.

"Changing into a wolf. It's the old superstition that there were once werewolves. Maybe they were your genetically labile people, Steve."

She shrugged. "Werewolves are fairy tales. This is science."

Rhoda said, "Maybe nature did create people who could change from man to wolf. It's a fascinating idea. Maybe you're just tracking down something nature has already done, Steve."

Steve waved it aside. "There's no point in that. What we've

(193)

done is to give Jack the ability to change, or we've freed that ability if it's latent in everyone." She tapped her fingernail against her teeth absently. "It throws some fascinating evolutionary concepts open, but never mind that now. Under great stress you reacted by changing your chromosomal pattern and with it your body. You changed into any form necessary for your survival."

"I'll have just a little more of the gravy," Allie said. "Rhoda, I think the turkey is too dry. Next time we must use aluminum foil."

"It steams it. It's just not the same as roasting," Rhoda said.

Jack nodded at Steve. "I figured that out, that I changed to survive, when I wasn't sure I was going mad."

Rhoda reached over and patted his arm and he smiled at her briefly. "But you weren't in danger when you changed to a wolf," she said. "It wasn't a matter of survival."

Steve brushed that aside. "But there was stress. That's the point. Great stress and emotional turmoil."

"I also figured out," Jack said slowly, "that in my chromosomes I carried patterns for all the species man had ever gone through in his evolutionary climb."

Steve looked up at him. "There's no evolutionary line from man to bird, or for that matter from man to wolf or shark. You underestimate your chromosomes."

"What do you mean?"

She shrugged. "Bird, shark, wolf—they're all at the end of a long evolutionary line, just as man is. Man doesn't have any birds in his ancestry. They separated into different branches back at the archaeopteryx or before. The birds are the end product of millions of years of evolution, and so are men, but they're different evolutions. The same is true of the wolf. The branch-off there was before the marmosets. Marmosets, lemurs, tarsiers—that's man's line. I forget what the wolf line is, but your theory is all shot—thank God."

"Why thank God?"

"Because of what we want." She put down her silverware. "Because of what we grey-eyed women, as you call us, want. No, Jack. I think you have an almost infinite series of possible DNA blueprints in your body."

"I don't understand that."

"It's not so difficult. You have the potential for all possible forms of DNA. Remember, none of them use more than two purines and two pyrimidines. It's the arrangement of the four in sequence that's infinite. Somehow, I'm not completely sure how, you have the ability to pattern your DNA after every life form. It's an evolutionary thing, I'm sure, but it's not necessarily a function of what's in your evolutionary background. I think every living creature has all these patterns, they have stored blueprints for all life as it has existed and as it will exist. Under certain circumstances they change. Maybe bursts of cosmic radiation caused the change in evolution. With you it's the chemicals I inoculated into you."

The concept staggered him and he shook his head. "I can't accept that. The storage alone would be impossible, the amount to be stored."

"That's the smallest part of it. One cell carries enough taped information to make a man. Have you any idea how many cells there are in your body, how many cells alone in the unused portion of your mind? No, storage is no problem. The problem of retrieval, however, is staggering. How could your mind ever retrieve those stored tapes or put them to work?"

"But it did? You think it did?"

"It did, and it will again." Steve toyed with her dessert as Rhoda and Allie cleared the table and brought out coffee. "Let me tell you about us."

"This I don't understand. How can I help you?"

Rhoda, with a sudden eagerness in her face, stopped on her way to the kitchen and said, "Do you mean that?"

Bewildered, he asked, "Mean what?"

Rhoda came back to the table. "Do you mean that you want to help us, that you will help us?"

Jack frowned. "That's not what I said. I said, how could I help you!"

Steve nodded. "I know that's what you meant. Let me tell you about ourselves. We are mutants, born with a telepathic ability, and with grey eyes linked to it. There are eighty genes involved, and at least one of them on the X chromosome."

Jack interrupted. "I don't know much about genetics, but I know that while a mutation of eighty genes may be possible, the mutation of the same eighty in more than one woman is hard to believe."

Steve smiled. "Flatly it's impossible. One gene mutated. I said eighty genes are involved, maybe more. The new gene causes telepathy and affects other genes which in turn affect our eye color, the laying down of pigment. There may be some skin effects associated with it that I haven't fully understood, and I'm sure that ear shape, in some way, is affected. You know, thare's a balance among genes. When one changes, the others change, sometimes in minor ways. The influence goes back and forth. The one mutant gene affects seventy-nine others that I'm sure of, maybe more. They modify eye color, but also the structure of the pineal gland. You know that in our evolutionary past the pineal gland was once a third eye."

"I've heard that, but the whole thing is bewildering."

"In us the pineal gland, I'm sure, is the organ of telepathy. The mutation of this one gene on the X chromosome has happened many times in history, I'm sure, but it's a recessive gene. You know what that means?"

"I think it means you must have two of them for it to work."

"That's about it, simplified. Blue eyes are recessive, and so is blond hair. If two blond-haired people marry, all their children will be blond. Since the gene is recessive, to be blond you must have two genes for blondness on matching chromosomes. Do you follow?"

He sipped his coffee. "Through a hazy fog, but go on."

"Genetically, we call having two matching genes like that being allelomorphic. Each of a human's chromosomes, incidentally, has a matching partner."

"Except the X chromosome, the one that determines sex."

"Right, and therein lies our problem."

Rhoda brought a bottle of brandy and four big-bellied snifters to the table. She looked questioningly at Jack and he nodded and took the glass, inhaling the deep, rich odor as he listened to Steve.

"Men have a Y chromosome as a partner for the X. Women have two X's. But the Y isn't as long as the X. Only part of it matches up. Because of that there are many genes on the X chromosome which aren't matched by ones on the Y. If they're dominant, they work anyway. If they're recessive, like the telepathy gene, they don't work in a man, even if he has one on his X chromosome."

"And he can never be allelomorphic for the genes that lie on the part of the X chromosome that is not matched by the Y."

"Right again. The gene that causes telepathy, our mutant gene, lies on that unmatched part of the X chromosome." She stared at her brandy glass, then looked up at Jack. "We have recognized what we are. We live with it proudly. It's the breath of life to us. With telepathy we have a closeness, a warmth and honesty that is beyond anything else on earth."

Rhoda took Jack's hand. "You know how many writers have used the alienation of man as a literary theme?"

Jack nodded. "It's very big in literature today."

"It is, and their solution, if any of them offer one, is always fumbling and inept. They offer love. Love becomes the only workable possibility, the only force that can break down the barriers between uninvolved humans. But it's not the real an-

(197)

swer, not the answer all of them are groping towards."

"And telepathy is?"

"Of course. I can't begin to describe the satisfaction, the completeness of two minds linked together. What speech is to the dumb, sound to the deaf, sight to the blind, telepathy is to those who can speak and see and hear."

Steve said, "It's everything to us, and yet we've never shared it with a man. Some of us fall in love, some of us marry and have children, but what the hell is the use? I can be closer to Allie and Rhoda with no physical contact than I could ever be to you in sexual intercourse."

The bluntness of it shocked him, and he started to protest, but Rhoda cut him short. "It's true, and because it's true real love, man and woman love, is impossible to us."

He looked at her intently and her eyes fell before his and she said softly, "There is of course love, and there is love. There are many different levels of love."

"You can never hate anyone with whom you have a telepathic bond," Steve said abruptly. "That's a strange outgrowth of telepathy. Hate, suspicion, fear, misinterpretation—all of them are meaningless terms among us. We form a league, a telepathic league, and we work together when we have to with complete cooperation because we know and understand each other so incredibly well. A telepathic human, Jack, could never wage war on another telepath, never commit a crime, never kill, murder or steal or hurt another telepath. It's just not possible. Nor could he deceive another telepath."

Jack sat there, turning his brandy glass, listening and in spite of all reason, believing. "But you can't reproduce," he said finally.

"If we marry a man with a normal X chromosome, our children will be normal. Telepathy is recessive. The girls of such a marriage will have one normal X chromosome and one with the mutant gene. Our sons will all have mutant genes on their X chromosomes."

(198)

Startled at the implications, he said, "If this mutation has been around for a long time, if you women do marry, then there must be a lot of hybrids in the world."

"There are," Steve said, "and they probably have the roughest time of all."

"Why?"

She shrugged. "They're neither fish nor fowl, neither completely normal nor completely telepathic."

"You mean they have some degree of telepathy?"

"The gene has some effect, even recessive. It does affect the pineal slightly, not enough to create a telepath, but enough to allow a man to broadcast telepathically under certain circumstances." She wet her lips. "When my father died he 'broke through' as we call it and cried out. He was a hybrid. He had to be, to have me."

"I see. And what are these hybrid men like?"

Steve shrugged. "Unfulfilled men. They sense something wrong, I think. They can sometimes almost put their finger on it, but never quite. It gives them a very peculiar empty relationship to life, as if they're always searching for something, for something they don't comprehend, for something they can never find. They're only half alive."

He lifted his eyes and stared for a moment at each of them. "And I'm like that? I'm one of these hybrids?"

Steve nodded. "I recognized it that first day in the lab. You're lucky. A lot of men, and women too, born like that take to dope, become alcoholics—many become writers, always questioning and searching within themselves for something they can sense but can't understand. I'd hate to do a chromosome count on some of the prophets and saviors."

"And a lot of us become bums," he said dully, "aimless people with no goal or direction."

Rhoda's hand touched his, and he gave her a crooked smile. "Only you've got a goal for me. Tell me."

Steve leaned across the table. "You thought you had the ability to become any creature in man's past. I tell you you have more than that. You can become any creature in man's future, in life's future. You became animals adjacent to man's evolutionary ladder. Now you can take a step up that ladder."

"You three," he nodded at them, "are what man is evolving into."

"Unfortunately," Steve said drily, "we are what woman is evolving into. You can become the first man allelomorphic for telepathy."

He frowned. "Right off I can see one flaw in your theory."

"What's that?"

He shrugged. "You said the mutation is on the X chromosome, I assume on the part not matched by the Y. How can you ever match it with another gene?"

Steve smiled. "That's good thinking, but it can be done, simply by extending the Y chromosome. The gene is not far from the section that matches. All it would take is a few meaningless genes with the mutant among them."

"Are you sure they'd be meaningless?"

"Maybe not. Maybe they'd turn you into a horned man. I don't know. But they'd be sex-linked. Only the men of the race would have them."

"I'd hate to end up with four legs or green skin." He laughed, and then smiled thoughtfully. "So I would become the father of what? Of all telepathic children of tomorrow?"

"Oh, I'm not saying humanity will be telepathic tomorrow, or even in a hundred or a thousand years. But eventually it will happen."

"How? Won't there always be nontelepaths?"

"It'll happen by natural selection, not by extinction, if that's on your mind. Always, all through evolution, when an extra survival factor occurs in a species by mutation, that factor becomes universal. It may take a few thousand years, but eventually it happens."

(200)

"And it will happen to humanity?"

"If we give it a start—by creating a father for our children."

"How many are you?" he asked, shaking his head. "I was never a . . ."

"A lover? A libertine?" Steve finished for him. "We're not asking you to be one. There's always artificial insemination. Why, with one orgasm you could probably fertilize the world!"

"That's a happy thought," Rhoda interrupted, pushing her chair back and standing up. "For that you can clear up, Steve. I'll show Jack the rest of the house."

He didn't particularly want to see the rest of the house, old and historic as it was, but he was glad of an excuse to escape from Steve, to try and sort out his own emotions, and he wanted to be alone with Rhoda.

He followed her through the kitchen, wood panelled and with an enormous hearth and fireplace, large enough to walk into and piled high with ashes. A great, blackened, cast-iron pot hung from a hook above the ashes. Beyond the kitchen a study, wood panelled too, showed the back of the brick hearth and another, smaller fireplace.

"The house is full of fireplaces," Rhoda said. "I guess it was the only heat available when it was built."

He caught her wrist. "I don't want an historical tour, Rhoda."

"What do you want, Jack?"

He let her hand fall. "I'm darned if I know. I guess I want to sort some sense out of this whole fantastic mess. I want some guarantee that I'll still be myself tomorrow and not some godforsaken animal."

"And if you become one of us, is that also a godforsaken animal?"

"Perhaps godforsaken is closer than you think." He threw himself down in one of the study chairs and pulled aside the curtain over the small window. It looked out on the rear of the

(201)

house and a pile of new lumber.

"What do you mean?"

He shrugged restlessly. "I don't know. If you're not human, you and Steve and Allie, the rest of your telepathic friends, what right have you got to human gods?"

She smiled and reached out to take his hand. "Is God for Homo sapiens alone?"

"What will tomorrow's man call himself, Homo telepathens?"

"He may just be a little closer to sapiens. We are the same as you, or any other woman or man. We can mate with men."

"But there is that mutant gene." He stood up abruptly and she held his hand, forcing him to turn towards her.

"Jack, what's wrong?"

"I don't know. Perhaps I'm scared. What guarantee do you have, any of you, that I'll change into what you want? And how are you going to make me change?"

She stood up and moved close to him, her grey eyes staring up at him luminously. "Do you want to change, Jack? That's what I think is most important of all. Do you want to?"

He took her in his arms but held his head back, staring down at her eyes. "Would you believe me if I told you that I loved you?"

"I've known you wanted me since we met in Montreal."

"I said loved, not wanted."

She searched his eyes, frowning. Then very softly she shook her head. "We are so vulnerable when we deal with men. It's like walking into a fog, into cobwebs. How do I know what you feel, Jack? How do I know what you're thinking?"

"Men have loved women since the race began without ever sharing their thoughts."

"But they weren't women like us." She reached up and touched his face. "How young you've become. You used to have wrinkles around your eyes and now they're gone."

"Did you mind those wrinkles?"

"I loved them."

He caught her finger and kissed it, then kissed her lips, gently at first, and then with a sudden surge of fierceness. Her lips were cool and closed but he forced them open with his tongue, touched her teeth and then her mouth. He felt her grow limp in his arms and she moved her head, crying out softly in protest.

She pulled away, her eyes wide, her parted lips red and bruised, and there was a mixture of confusion and longing on her face. "Oh, Jack, Jack . . . if I could only reach you, only hear your mind!"

The room was almost dark then, a soft blue light reaching in from the small window. Behind them they could hear the rattling of pots in the kitchen and occasionally Steve's voice.

"My mind, my mind!" He turned away from her. "I offer you my heart and you ask for my mind." He shook his head. "Is this a part of the test, Rhoda? Am I supposed to change now? Is this the stress Steve talked about?"

She didn't answer, and when he turned back she was standing there, her hands covering her face. "That wasn't fair."

"I'm sorry." He went to her contritely and took her hands from her face. Her cheeks were wet with tears and he kissed them very gently. "I didn't mean any of that. Of course I'll go through with the test, whatever it is."

The noise from the kitchen had stopped and abruptly he asked, "Can they hear us, Steve and Allie? Can they hear any of this?"

She smiled through her tears. "Can you hear someone when they don't speak?"

"Is it like that?"

She nodded, "And I haven't spoken."

She brushed her cheeks dry, then abruptly said, "Come on. I'll show you the rest of the house."

There were two more rooms on the ground floor, a small

sewing room and a sun porch. On the floor above there were three bedrooms, and at the end of a long hall a single door, a peculiar door, solid, but obviously put in very recently. In the center of the door was a large round metal dial with an arrow. Numbers from 1 to 25 circled the dial.

Rhoda stepped up to it and spun the dial. "We just put this in."

Frowning, Jack pulled the door open. There were two flush bolts and the side of the door showed as raw metal. Open, it gave on a small balcony with a flight of iron steps leading to the ground.

"What the hell is this?" It seemed completely out of character with the rest of the house.

"A fire door." Rhoda shut it and spun the dial. "Burglar-proof too. It's locked now. It's a combination lock, and only Allie, Steve and I know the combination."

"It doesn't make much sense for a fire door."

"Eventually we'll replace all of the doors with these, only Steve says they'll look nicer, old-fashioned."

"But if they're fire doors and someone doesn't know the combination . . ."

"We all know it, and if one forgets it, we can broadcast it to her mentally. Come on." She caught at his arm and pulled him towards the hall.

"I don't know the combination."

"We'll tell it to you, or better yet, leave the door open while you're here. Here's the guest room."

It was a small bedroom a few feet from the fire door. Beyond it the hall stretched for about 20 feet before it reached the bathroom and the other two bedrooms and stairway. Jack looked into the room and smiled. Three tiny windows, shaped like portholes on a ship, faced the low hills, almost invisible now in the darkness. There was a small bed against one wall, and a tiny sink and wardrobe. The room was decorated to look like the

(204)

cabin of a ship, even to a whaling lantern that hung from the ceiling.

"Cute?" She pointed to the lantern. "Steve actually wanted it to swing back and forth with a little motor, but I thought that would make our guests seasick."

Jack smiled. "It's cute, all right, but what's the point?"

"I guess someone was a boat fancier. It came with the house. Let me show you our room. It has an unbelievable view, even at night."

Later, back in the living room, Allie had put out a bowl of fruit and cheese and Steve was busy peeling an orange in one continuous strip. "If it's done right," she grinned as they came in, "the fruit sits on the peel as if on a big spring. Come on. Sit down and relax."

Jack sat at the table and took a pear. "I should be getting back to the city."

"Nonsense. You'll sleep over. We'll give you the captain's room. This is Friday night. Tomorrow I'll drive you into town. All right?"

"Please stay, Jack." Rhoda took his hand and he smiled at her.

"Okay. Now let's talk some more genetics. Maybe I can puzzle some of this out."

"Fire away." Steve finished the orange and set it on its peel where it bounced up and down. "Genetics it is."

Chapter Fifteen

Jᴀᴄᴋ ᴡᴏᴋᴇ out of a sound sleep to feel a hand shaking him, and then, as he struggled to sit up, fingers were placed on his mouth. "Shh!"

"Rhoda?" He reached for the bedside light as the dark form bending over him drew back. "Is that you?"

"It's Clifford, Jack."

"Clifford? What the hell are you doing here?" He fumbled for the switch. "Wait a minute. Let me put on the lamp."

"Can anyone see it?"

"What's the difference?" He switched on the bed lamp and stared at Clifford in the circle of light. "What time is it? What are you doing here? Who let you in?"

"At least your eyes aren't grey." Clifford sat down on the bed with a sigh. "No one let me in. I've been creeping about like a thief in the night. I rented a car and came up here this evening. I parked down the road and waited in the woods till the lights went out. Christ, I'm tired and hungry and stiff as a board."

"Well, come downstairs and I'll rassle you up a sandwich. There's plenty of food left over."

Clifford let out his breath in a harsh laugh. "You think they'd feed me if they caught me here?"

"They, they? There's Rhoda and Steve and Allie. That's all. What is this all about?"

Suddenly Clifford reached up and tilted the lamp, then pulled the bedclothes back. Jack had been sleeping in his underwear, and there was a long pause as Clifford stared at his body. "Have they . . . changed you already? Jack—" He shook his head in bewilderment. "What is it? You're different."

"Cliff—" He sat up. "What time is it?"

"After three."

"Have you got a smoke, a cigar or a cigarette?" He lit it after Clifford silently handed him one and he drew in a deep breath, then coughed and swore silently. Finally he looked at the cigarette. "I ought to give this up. At least now I can be afraid of cancer. It's cured, you know. Steve is positive."

"Jack, what's happened? Where have you been?"

"I tried to commit suicide, Cliff. I jumped off the George Washington Bridge, only it didn't work. I guess I wanted to live out whatever life was left me. It's a long, crazy story, Cliff, like becoming a wolf. I changed into a bird, and then, when I was too heavy to fly and hit the water, into a shark." Briefly he told Clifford what had happened. "And that explains this body," he finished lamely, "or does it?"

Clifford shook his head. "I feel like Alice halfway down the rabbit hole. I don't believe any of this and yet I do. They chased me all over New York yesterday, your grey-eyed telepaths, trying to keep me from warning you."

"Warning me about what?"

"About what they intend to do. They intend to change you, Jack, to make you one of them, to put you through some kind of test that will make you change into a telepath."

"But I know that, Cliff. That's the whole point of it. I haven't really agreed to go through with it yet. Maybe I've half promised, but we haven't discussed it."

"What makes you think they need your agreement?"

"What? Cliff, you've got them wrong. They're decent, normal human beings, a hell of a lot more decent than most. I told Steve I'd sleep on it. I don't have to go through with the test, whatever it is."

"Don't you? Look, Jack, Steve is no fool and no innocent. I don't know how decent any of them are. They want you to help reproduce their kind, to replace human beings."

"Sure, in a few thousand years, and what's so bad about replacing us? Haven't we made enough of a mess of things? Cliff, don't be so melodramatic. You just don't know them."

"I know them better than you do. I've had some experience with them. Wait!" He reached out and switched off the light. "Did you hear something?"

They were both silent, listening, but nothing broke the quiet of the sleeping house. Finally Clifford relaxed. "Anyway, leave the light off. Jack, did you talk to Steve about how they expect you to change, about the test?"

"No, because I haven't decided to go through with it yet."

"They stopped me from seeing you today, or was it yesterday? They were afraid I'd warn you."

"Didn't you call me and speak to Rhoda? Didn't you have an assignment? A last minute thing?"

"No."

"But Rhoda said you did."

"Well, she lied. And doesn't that tell you something? Why was it so necessary that they get you up here without my seeing you first?"

He thought of Rhoda's kisses. Had the test already started without the bother of consent? What was the force needed to make him change? Hadn't he once tried to sort out the ground rules. Was it simply stress, or what?

As if reading his mind Clifford said, "You changed to save your life. Suppose they put you into a situation where you had to either change into a telepath or die?"

"They wouldn't!"

"Wouldn't they? Two of them held guns to me yesterday and they were playing for keeps. They meant it."

Abruptly he thought of the fire door, the meaningless combination lock. *We all know it*, Rhoda had said, *and even if we forget, we can broadcast it to each other telepathically.* Had there been a peculiar intensity in the way she had said that, in the way she had repeated it?

He groaned abruptly, less because of his safety, the threat to his own life, than because of the betrayal the whole thing implied. Then all the talk of a telepath's inability to deceive— but of course, they had been careful to say another telepath.

"I didn't think they'd let you know that," Clifford was saying. "Their plan couldn't work unless they kept it from you, and I don't think your death matters that much."

He shook his head. "They're not like that," he protested stubbornly. "I don't believe they'd risk my life." But even as he protested he knew he wasn't sure. There was still that terrible doubt, and what was the combination door for? They were desperate and this was quite possibly their only chance.

"You've got to get out of here, Jack. This whole house isn't right. I can just sense it. I don't even like the way I was able to reach you, none of the doors even locked. It's all too easy." He stood up and walked to the porthole windows, pulling the cur-

(209)

tains aside to look out at the moon-swept hills. "They might be out there now for all we know." He frowned at the windows. "Why are these so small? A man couldn't fit through them."

Jack stared at him. "A man couldn't fit through them," he whispered slowly, and he remembered the long hallway and the fire door, this room at the end and the only exit the door with the combination lock. This wing of the building was a trap. A specially constructed trap. He had seen a pile of raw wood outside today. Had they just built this wing?

He jumped out of bed and started pulling on his pants. "We're going to have it out right now," he said. "We'll wake up Steve and Rhoda and find out what's at the bottom of this."

Clifford didn't answer him. He had lifted his head, his nostrils spread, sniffing the air. "Jack! I smell smoke!"

Buttoning his pants Jack ran to the door and pulled it open, then fell back coughing as a cloud of smoke billowed into the room. "God damn it, we're too late! Shut the window quick. The house is on fire!"

"Let's get out of here." Clifford stared around the room frantically. "The windows are too small. We'll be trapped in a minute. Come on. The corridor!"

Jack opened the door again and they ran out into the corridor. The fire was down the hall, between them and the other bedrooms and stairway. A sheet of flame engulfed the entire corridor, sealing them effectively into this wing. Behind them was the steel door with the combination lock.

Clifford grabbed two washcloths and soaked them with water at the tiny sink while Jack stood hypnotized by the flames. Shoving one at Jack he said, "Wake up! Don't be a fool. Hold it over your nose. Can we make a run for it?"

He shuddered. "Through that? Never." He turned and stared at the door. "That's the only way."

"Well, come on. We'll break it down if we have to." Holding the wet cloth to his mouth, choking and coughing, Clifford

(210)

stumbled down the hall to the door and pushed against it.

Jack came up behind him, looking over his shoulder at the fire. He should be worried about Rhoda. If not Steve and Allie, at least Rhoda. Had the fire sealed them off too? But that was still pretending, pretending that this was not all deliberate, not a trap cunningly contrived to force the issue—change or die!

Clifford had been right. He had been a stupid dupe all along, and now this! And Clifford caught along with him. That must be part of the plan, added pressure. He felt a wave of fury and anger. Damn them! Let him just get out of here and he'd show them, oh, Christ!

He pushed Clifford aside and tugged at the door, then threw himself against it with all his force. It held rigid and he bounced back with a stinging pain in his shoulder. Clifford, staring at him wildly over the wet cloth cried, "Let's both try." Knowing the futility of it they both flung themselves against the door, again and again, but outside of bruising their bodies they made no impact. The door was locked. The steel wouldn't give.

Jack spun the dial, cursing savagely. They couldn't do this. They'd have to open it from outside. They couldn't risk two deaths! Clifford had darted back to the room and he staggered out with a chair and pushing Jack aside started slamming it against the steel.

Why hadn't he gotten the combination from Rhoda, he thought frantically. But she would never have given it to him. Then why had he stayed, why? Why?

We all know it. If one forgets we can broadcast it to her.

All right, accept the trap, become telepathic or die! He saw Clifford sink to his knees, coughing desperately as the smoke ate at his lungs. It was billowing along the ceiling, great clouds of it, and behind them they could hear the sharp crackling of the fire.

"Pound the door," Clifford gasped. Jack grabbed the chair and slammed it against the door till it smashed in his hands.

(211)

The acrid smoke bit at his eyes and raw, terrible, animal fear filled him and anger, a raging flood of anger. Change to what? What animal could survive fire? But change, change or die! And he felt the slipping of his flesh, the lengthening of his bones, sprouting feathers.

From the floor Clifford stared up in growing horror and screamed, "No, No!" as realization struck him. "For Christ's sake, not a *phoenix!*"

Clifford pulled at him desperately, screaming in his ear above the roar of the fire. "A telepath, you stupid bastard, a telepath, not a goddamned phoenix!"

It was Clifford's life too that was at stake, Jack realized dimly, through his altered brain. He must change so that they could both survive or it was no good, no good at all. Abruptly, as realization sank in, the bones shifted, grew solid again and the feathers drew in on themselves, some falling off. The fantastic, birdlike form he had started to become resolved itself back to a man and he knew that he was changing again, a man and yet more than a man.

And then, even as a searing wave of flame reached out to them, he broke through, his mind pushing aside the curtains of soft webbing that separated him from the others, the three women waiting so desperately on the balcony behind the door. *Forward three, back twelve, forward two.* It pushed in on his raw, newly changed mind, over and over, behind a desperate sobbing and pleading. *Hear us, oh, hear us!*

His fingers turned the dial, already warm from the fire, turned it again and then a third time, and with a thrust of his shoulders the door swung open and he stumbled out on the balcony, then turned back to pull Clifford's unconscious form after him.

In the darkness he heard their voices, and yet not voices, so soft, so much a part of his mind. *Here, this way, darling. Oh, thank heaven, thank heaven!* The gentle, tender touch of

Rhoda's fear, anxiety and love, such loving solicitude and gratitude, and Steve's strength, iron-hard strength and blind, driving
will, and Allie, motherly tears reaching out to comfort and
hold . . .

And his own anger and fury at the betrayal, at the falseness of
their deceit blazed out of him as he lifted Clifford gently and
started down the metal steps to the ground. *If he's hurt . . .*

No, no. It's only the smoke. He'll be all right. Reassurance.
Comfort.

But he might have died! What kind of monsters are you?

And you might have died too. Steve's thoughts, the quiet
pride of accomplishment. Was this Steve, this incredibly calm,
strong mind, a will that was implacable and yet just, a firm, un-
swerving conviction of her own right? *In war there are risks.*

We were never your soldiers. Liars. Cheats.

And from Rhoda an assurance if he had died, she would have
died too, that night, a knife in her belt, against her heart. She
couldn't lie, not on this level. He knew and accepted her statement. But what right did they have to dare do this?

Clifford was sitting up, gulping fresh air in deep breaths. Behind them the house billowed clouds of smoke from the open
door while yellow tongues of flame licked up the white siding.

Jack pulled him to his feet. "Let's get away from here. Can
you walk?"

"Yes." He took a few steps and winced. "I'm not too steady."

"Where's your car? I want to get you to a hospital."

Behind them, with a crash, the end of the corridor fell out.
The rest of the house was still untouched, but this wing was a
mass of flames. Steve touched his arm and handed him the key to
her MG. "Take my car. It's right here in the driveway."

They stood watching as he helped Clifford into the car, ignoring the fire behind them, stood silently as he turned on the ignition, shifted into gear and raced down the driveway and into the
road. In the distance he heard the whine of fire sirens, and men-

tally questioned, *It was all prepared?*

Necessity, absolute. We knew it would happen. Regret. The courage and strength to go through with it from Steve, and from Rhoda, *Come back, Jack. I love you.* Implicit truth. Sincerity. Honesty. And Allie, *God bless you!* How typical, like a slice of thick apple pie, like roast turkey and buttered carrots. Allie would always be that homely, that warm and simple, telepathic or not. And he answered them savagely, with a mental blaze of resentment, anger, disillusionment, bitterness.

Beside him Clifford shook himself like a wet dog and wound down the window, gulping in great mouthfuls of the night air. "I'm all right, Jack. I don't need any hospital."

"Still, we ought to have you checked." They were on Route 23 now, headed for the city. "We can stop off at the first town."

"No, believe me. Let's go back and get my car."

Savagely, "I don't want to go back. I'll take you to the city in this. I can get the car tomorrow, today. . . .what time is it?"

"All right." He was too weak to protest. "I think it's almost four." He shivered. "Has this car got a heater?"

By the light of the dashboard Jack fiddled with the dials. "There. It's on."

Clifford caught his hand as he drew it back, then in a tight voice said, "Can you turn on the overhead light?"

"Sure. Why?" He flicked the switch and turned to face Clifford. "What is it?"

Clifford stared at him for a moment, then wet his lips. "Your eyes are grey."

Jack looked ahead at the road, and after a moment he smiled. "I thought they would be."

"And your skin is gold."

"Gold!" Startled, he looked at his hand. "My God, you're right." What had Steve said about linked genes, those few extra on the Y chromosome? *Steve?* On the mental waveband he called out, *Can you hear me?*

(214)

Very faint her voice answered, *"Is Clifford all right?"*

He sent a picture of Clifford sitting beside him. From Steve gratitude, relief, pleasure. He thought of the house and a picture of it came back, *the wing gutted, the fire out and the rest still standing.*

You were right about linked genes on the Y chromosome. Golden skin, grey eyes.

Faintly, they were almost at the limits of transmission, Steve's surprise, question. Other changes? Ears?

He reached up to feel their pointed tops, like a double lobe. A picture of a complicated DNA molecule came from Steve, and suddenly he understood the genetic mechanics, the section of DNA, of double helix affected by the mutant gene, his own changed Y chromosome.

Beside him Clifford stirred and coughed. "Are you all right?" Jack asked.

"Yes. Just shaken up, and cold. Christ, I'm cold."

He pulled his head over and touched his own cheek to Clifford's forehead. A sudden memory of years ago, lifetimes ago, raced unbidden through his mind. He had sat on the edge of his daughter's bed and he had felt her forehead this way, had sat with her in the dimly lit bedroom while she tossed and whimpered with a childhood fever. He thought of Anita, his wife. It had been all wrong, so wrong, and now he suddenly knew, with a frightening clarity, just where and how it had gone wrong, what he had never known how to do.

"You're all right, Cliff." He ran his hand affectionately over Clifford's bald head. "I never thanked you for getting into this."

Clifford laughed, but with a faint undercurrent of hysteria. "If I hadn't been with you, do you know what you would have turned into?"

"What?"

"A phoenix, a goddamned mythical phoenix! What a laugh that would have been, a myth instead of their new man. What a

(215)

way to start a civilization, with a ready-made myth."

"Cliff, stop it."

"All right." He was silent for a long time and they raced down Route 23 to the Hawthorne Circle and then on towards the city. "What I don't understand," he said finally, "is how you could have changed into a phoenix. There's no such thing. There just isn't."

What had Steve told him? There are blueprints for every life form that ever was or will be—was that true or was that only part of the truth? For every life form that man has ever conceived of, griffins and hippogriffs and centaurs and sphinxes! Oh, God!

Steve! He cried out on the mental band, and dimly, sleepily, a voice answered. Not Steve. A girl in bed in Riverdale, stirred out of dreams by his call, turned, stretched luxuriantly silky legs, switched on a light, and he saw her image in the mirror beside her bed. Black hair in a soft cloud over a delicate mulatto face, grey eyes and a pink tongue touching her teeth. *Greetings, hello.* Affection tinged with lazy desire. *You're Jack Freeman.*

Sorry I woke you.

Stretching yawning, sleep clouded with curiosity, interest. *Not at all. So it worked. Oh great, great!* Excitement cutting through the languor. *I want to see you, Jack!*

To his surprise he answered with a flood of warmth, sexual warmth, affection, a promise, sometime soon.

My name is Marie Wilson. Desire, affection, interest, sexual interest.

None of it could be hidden, he realized with a mixture of delight and fear. Were the last barriers down? And yet how quickly they had understood each other, how little need for subterfuge or deception. He would sleep with her someday. They both knew it and she had turned off the light, gone back to sleep.

Was it always to be like this? With a rush of foreboding he

(216)

whispered, "I can't be expected to give up every defense!"

Clifford, dozing next to him, sat up suddenly. "What?"

"Nothing." He slowed to pay the toll, and then entered Manhattan. At Clifford's building he helped him out of the car. "Are you all right?" The city was grey with the promise of dawn.

"Tired, exhausted. I feel as if I've been wallowing in smoke and soot and as if I've been through a wringer, but I'm all right. Oh, sure!"

"I'm sorry, Cliff." He followed him inside and up to his apartment. "Have you got a cup of coffee? I'm going to take the car back now."

"I'll go with you."

He shook his head. "No. Just give me the car keys. Cliff, I've got to go alone." His anger, his fury had died away. "There are too many unsettled problems."

Clifford started a pot of coffee while Jack walked to the mirror and studied his face. His features hadn't changed, but the skin was gold, a light gold. Could he pass for mulatto? Probably. He didn't have the features to be oriental, but the skin color wasn't oriental either, or Negro, or anything he had ever seen before. Looking at himself he realized that he was without a shirt and barefoot. He'd have to borrow clothes from Clifford.

A touch of color on his pants caught his eye, and he picked it off. It was a tiny feather, green and gold and red, a phoenix feather, the only one in the world!

"They're monsters, Jack," Clifford came up behind him. "You can't go back there. They're capable of anything. They want a stud for their children, that's all."

"A stud? Oh, no, no!" The warmth of their minds, the honesty, the tragedy behind Steve's iron will, Rhoda's tenderness and love, the girl in Riverdale. "They want much more, Cliff. You can't begin to understand."

"You're the one who doesn't understand. They have you bulldozed."

(217)

"No. You see, we can't lie to each other, none of us. That's what you don't understand. I left full of anger and hate, but I have to go back. I have to work that out. You see, I belong with them."

Clifford, staring at him, reached out and touched his ears. "They're pointed," he said irrelevantly. "Phoenixes and leprechauns, Jesus Christ!" He shook his head and went into the kitchen, returning with two cups of coffee. "At least stay over. If you're as exhausted as I am, you shouldn't drive."

Jack gulped the coffee. "Get some sleep and I'll see you when I bring the car back. I want to check out what Steve told me about the cancer with some doctor at Sloan-Kettering. I think she's right, that I'm cured, but I want a checkup."

Staring at him, Clifford said, "There's no telling what else they'll find. Grey eyes, gold skin and pointy ears. Are you still human, Jack?"

"The male of the species." He grinned. "Homo telepathens!"

Clifford sipped his coffee, then sighed. "I'll get you a shirt and shoes. A goddamned Phoenix, how about that?"

"Here." Jack handed him the feather.

"What is it?"

"The only phoenix feather in the world."

Cliff took it and turned it slowly in his hands. "I'll hold onto it. Goodbye, Jack."

Downstairs Jack stood for a moment alongside the car and looked up the silent, deserted street. Suddenly on the mental band he cried out with a wild eager soundless shout, *Hello all of you. Hello. Greetings. Good morning. Awake.*

Faintly at first, stirring out of sleep, surprise, delight, amazement, and so many awake waiting for just this, a ripple of joy. *It worked. Jack!* And then voice after voice, *Greetings. Welcome.* Tearful and eager and delighted, accepting, enfolding, joy, joy! One by one, a legion of them, thankful, tearful happy.

Happiness like a comfortable flood. *Welcome!*

(218)

He drove crosstown through a silent city ringing with mental calls of welcome, never alone again, and he headed uptown. The girl in Riverdale, a woman in Yonkers, two teen-age sisters in White Plains, and then the long highway to South Salem.

Steve? Rhoda? I'm coming back!

The early sun touched the road with pink and the sky lightened to green-blue and gold and white. And then their thoughts reached out and welcomed him. Confidence, sureness from Steve, calm and strong. *You made me a promise once, Jack.*

I remember. Sexuality, laughter, challenge.

And Rhoda, as soft and tender as a caress. *My darling. Forgive.*

Assent, love, impatience.

And Allie, putting up biscuits in a fire-blackened kitchen. The house still stood. It could be fixed, but meanwhile Allie had breakfast to prepare.

His people. His women!